Clara's Daughter

MEIKE ZIERVOGEL grew up in the north of Germany and came to London in 1986 to study Arabic. She has worked as a journalist for Reuters and Agence France-Presse. In 2008 she founded Peirene Press, an award-winning, London-based independent publishing house. Her debut novel *Magda* was shortlisted for the *Guardian*'s Not the Booker prize and nominated as a book of the year 2013 by the *Irish Times*, *Observer* and *Guardian* readers. Meike lives in London with her husband and two children. Find out more about Meike at www.meikeziervogel.com.

Clara's Daughter
Meike Ziervogel

S
SALT

CROMER

PUBLISHED BY SALT

12 Norwich Road, Cromer, Norfolk NR27 0AX United Kingdom

First published by Salt Publishing, 2014

Printed in Great Britain by Clays Ltd, St Ives plc

Typeset in Paperback 9.5/15

ISBN 978 1 907773 79 2 paperback

1 3 5 7 9 8 6 4 2

'She rises up out of the water and steps over the shingle, keeping the same calm pace.'
JAN VAN MERSBERGEN, *Tomorrow Pamplona*

Clara's Daughter

1

THERE ARE NO cars on the road this early on a Saturday morning. The leaves on the huge plane trees around the old village green rustle in the light breeze. A refreshing chill from the night still lingers in the air. Jim slows down, steers his bicycle into the middle of the empty road and waits for Michele to catch up, looking back over his shoulder. With her strawberry-blonde hair hanging loose beneath the helmet, her summer skirt and green cardigan, she looks just like the young woman he first fell in love with twenty-five years ago. She arrives beside him, slightly flushed from pedalling uphill. She smiles. Jim stretches out his arm and she takes the offered hand. They ride towards Hampstead Heath together, hand in hand.

At the bottom of Merton Lane they chain their bikes to the railings. With swimming bags over their shoulders, they set off across the Heath. The anglers in their tents around the pond are still asleep. Two ducks stretch their necks, flap their wings, then gather speed and move across the water before taking off into the air. Michele's hand in Jim's feels soft and warm.

The gates to the mixed bathing pond are closed and a handwritten sign announces that *Due to lack of staff the pond will open at 10 a.m. on Saturday*. They exchange a mischievous glance and climb over the fence. The water is cold, but Jim dives straight in. As he resurfaces, he roars with pain and joy and threatens to splash Michele, who hasn't yet made it beyond the second rung of the ladder. She wets her arms and descends into the pond. She gasps for air, shrieking. She swims towards him and they hug, pressing their cold lips together, laughing, then quickly letting go of each other before they sink. They race to the end of the pond, turn around and race back. Michele wins. But only because Jim lets her. She pushes him underwater and speedily climbs the ladder on to the jetty to escape his retaliation.

'I've been thinking,' he says while towelling his body dry, 'now that Felix is at university too, why don't we sell the house, downsize to a flat and buy a small cottage up in Scotland?'

Michele is already dressed. She brushes her hair.

'I'm not in control of my own time,' she replies in a preoccupied voice. Then continues: 'As you know.

And I wouldn't be able to commit to going up there. Perhaps in a few years.' The spikes of her brush get stuck in a hair knot. 'And there is also my mother,' she adds, pulling the brush forcefully through the knot.

Jim steps into his trousers.

'You've been CEO for fifteen months now. Surely soon you'll be able to claim at least your weekends back and perhaps even take a couple of weeks' holiday.'

'Not if the Sea Shelf 3 deal comes through.'

She cleans the hair out of the brush and examines it. There are a few grey strands. She really ought to go to the hairdresser. She opens the palm of her hand and lets the wind take the fluffy ball. Jim watches it catch in a spider's web that is hanging between the branches of a hawthorn.

The patio in the back garden is sun-drenched. They lay breakfast outside and sit next to each other on the bench. Jim's laptop stands open on the table. He shows Michele a cottage on Barra, where they spent their honeymoon. She places her head on his shoulder and closes her eyes. The vibration of his deep voice enters her body and she breathes in his smell – a mix of cold pond water still lingering on his skin, sweat from cycling on his shirt and only a very faint trace of aftershave. This is how he smells when they are on their hiking holidays: a smell of distant places, adventures, physical exhaustion. She puts an arm around him. His body feels solid and strong. He continues talking but she is no longer listening. Her hand slides beneath his shirt and moves across the firm, smooth skin of his back. She lifts her head and places tender little kisses on his neck, travelling slowly upwards to his ear. He has fallen silent. Michele hears his breathing. He hasn't shaved yet, and the stubble rubs gently against her cheek. The fingers of her other hand dance teasingly across his tummy just above the waistline. He kisses her.

'Let's go upstairs,' he whispers.

She nods.

They step inside the kitchen. Jim turns around and kisses her again. His hands move down her back. Michele closes her eyes. He pushes her slowly towards the worktop and lifts her up on to the surface. She wraps her legs around his waist and pulls him close. Her hands glide upwards along the back of his head; her tongue meets his while she feels his hands on her skin. He unhooks her bra. For a moment he sucks gently on her earlobe. Goosebumps spread down her body. She giggles. She leans back and undoes the first buttons of her blouse. Jim's mouth is playing with her hard nipple. She pulls bra and blouse over her head. As she emerges from under her clothes, she opens her eyes.

For a split second her gaze falls over Jim's bent body on to the wall behind the kitchen table. The clock shows five to ten. The red second hand shifts towards the twelve. Her mother. She has to take her mother to the osteopath this morning. She quickly closes her eyes again. She had a funny feeling when she mentioned her mother earlier – as if there was something she ought to remember. Jim is now sucking her right nipple with slightly too much force. It hurts. The appointment is at eleven. Even today, on a Saturday morning, it will take more than three-quarters of an hour down to Battersea, and then there's the palaver of getting her mother out of the house – that's at least another fifteen minutes. She shakes her head involuntarily. She bends forward and lifts Jim's face. She kisses him, her hands unbuckling his belt. Hilary will be livid if their mother misses this appointment. Mum has recently started to complain of an increased pain in her knee and this was the first appointment her sister could arrange. Hilary is so stressed with her twins that frankly Michele would prefer to avoid creating any unnecessary friction. She might just about make it if she leaves right now. Jim is pushing her skirt up, moving the crotch of her pants aside. His actions have lost all sexiness; they feel crude. Michele is about to unzip his trousers, but then stops herself. She shifts her head back from Jim's face.

'I forgot. I have to take Mum to the osteopath today. In fact, in an hour. I really need to go.' She places her hand flat on his chest.

'Your mother can wait a few minutes,' he says, wanting to kiss her breast again.

'I'm sorry. I'm not in the mood any more. My brain has switched itself on.' She gives him a gentle push.

For a moment he hesitates. His hands are resting on her inner thighs.

'We'll make love tonight,' she says.

Suddenly he takes a step back. He will not beg. He zips up his trousers and buckles his belt. Michele jumps down from the worktop and puts on bra and blouse. Jim turns towards the kettle to make fresh coffee.

'What are your plans for the afternoon?' Michele asks, already in the hallway, searching in her swimming bag for the keys.

'I have a cricket match.'

'It's the Peels' dinner party tonight.'

'I haven't forgotten. It's a home match, so I should be back in time.'

He steps outside and fetches the cafetière. Michele grabs her handbag.

'Bye,' she calls over her shoulder, as she is pulling the front door shut behind her.

Jim is standing in the middle of the lawn with a steaming cup of coffee in his hand. They haven't made love in weeks. And over the past fifteen months, ever since Michele accepted the new job at Nordic Oil, they've managed a handful of times at most. He puts down the coffee and picks up an old cricket ball that is left lying around for the neighbours' cat to play with. She's too tired, she's too preoccupied, or she's not there at all. Perhaps he should have made a move as soon as they came back and not waited for her to take the initiative. Unwittingly, a sarcastic snort escapes from his nose. He's been rebuffed too often recently. This wasn't the first time that she'd stopped mid-flow, either. He weighs the ball in his right hand. Oddly enough, when the children were young it seemed easier: they booked a babysitter regularly, went out on dates, just the two of them, and made love afterwards. Or simply: had sex. Good solid sex. He swings his arm in a wide bowling motion and lets the ball drop a few metres in front of him at the edge of the lawn. He turns back to the table and closes the laptop. And when his wife isn't preoccupied with work, she is preoccupied with her mother. He leafs through Saturday's *Guardian* and pulls out the sport section. True, his mother-in-law has been a worry ever since Michele's father died a couple of years ago. The good news is, however, that Clara will go to a residential home soon. They found a very nice one six months back, not far away on the other side of the Heath. The home called last week to say that a place had become available.

His eyes fall on the headline: *Australia retains grip*. Jim shakes his head. He starts reading.

2

MICHELE – ONE WEEK LATER

I TAKE A pencil and snap it in half, just because I have to do something. I can't sit here and do nothing. Then I am still, and the house is still, and I know it wasn't enough simply to break a pencil. I want to do more. So I take the metal pen holder, turn slightly on my chair and throw it straight through the open door across the balcony and into the garden. The clattering noise as it hits the patio tells me I have achieved my aim. I get to my feet and pick up the two cushions from the chair and fling them into the garden too. Then I stop and consider the neighbours and wonder what they must be thinking, seeing our stuff flying through the air. Then I shrug my shoulders. What they are thinking is probably exactly right, namely that their neighbours are a middle-aged couple whose children have now left home, that she works far too hard and loves her job and the status and the illusion of power that it gives her far too much, that he is an attractive man whose career has stagnated over the last however many years, but actually he is the one who knows that there are far more important – or, at least, other equally important – things in life, that he has been such a great father to his kids and such an accommodating husband . . . No. Stop it. He hasn't been such an accommodating husband. He cared for the children while I went to work, but that had nothing to do with being accommodating, which suggests an element of sacrifice. Far from it. It suited him perfectly. He doesn't like to work 24/7, is happy with his part-time teaching, loves his cricket and fishing and fresh air far too much. Not to mention his naps during the day. I look around the room. I want to throw more stuff out of the window. My eyes are scanning the bookshelves. I can already see my arm stretching out and emptying the shelves with one huge sweep. No, not the books. Definitely not the books. I would regret it and have to spend hours afterwards putting them back. It's not that I am out of my mind with rage. I am simply angry and want to throw a fit. Like a toddler who hurls herself to the floor to show the whole world how angry and upset she is. And since I am too old to throw myself to the floor, I might as well throw something else. My eyes move across the desk. Paper, Sellotape, nail varnish. Too light, too inconspicuous. It needs to feel solid when I hurl it. There is a small coffee table in front of me. From the table my gaze goes down to my feet. I slip out of my sandals and fling first one and then the other into the garden. There and there. You've got it.

I am no longer worried about the neighbours. To tell the truth, part of me wouldn't mind them seeing my display of anger. Yes, in fact I have a right to be angry if my stupid husband goes and fucks a woman probably half my age, and, for that matter, his. What am I supposed to do? React with understanding? Show sympathy? Compliment him first, then give constructive criticism? Fuck him. No way. I storm out of the study and into the bedroom. I theatrically tear open the doors to his part of the wardrobe, both sides at once. My arms are open wide, the doors are open wide. There are a couple of suits hanging on the rail. Wonder when he wore them last. On the shelves underneath are his shirts, his thick woollen jumpers, his T-shirts, his sports clothes. I scoop up his beloved cricket whites and carry them to the balcony. I stand at the railings with the whites in my arms, as if holding a baby. I see my sandals on the grass, a couple of pens on the grey stone of the terrace. I lift the clothes over the railings, ready to drop them into the garden. For a few seconds I don't move. Then I turn around, go back into the study and sit down on one of the chairs – only to jump up again the next moment. If I remain sitting I will start to analyse what's happening and the anger will abate. But the sudden adrenalin rush was doing me good. I enjoyed it.

I shake my head. All my life I've been able to control my anger. That's why I am successful at my job. I have never lost my temper with anyone. Even the most useless people. I have learned to avoid them or, if I can't avoid them, to do their job for them. And nowadays I am in a position either to delegate their jobs to someone more efficient or to move them on. Nicely, kindly, even with a few compliments on the way. A lot of people don't want to get better at their jobs, aren't humble enough to improve, to learn. There is no point losing my temper. You run a business despite all the obstacles and inefficiencies of other people. It's a game. A mind game, a chess game, a game of endurance, an exhilarating game. Most difficulties you face aren't personal. And even the betrayals, the jealousies, the back-stabbings – you just have to try to see them coming and manoeuvre your way through; or

forgive yourself if you don't see them coming, draw
your lesson from them and move on. I sit down again.

But this is not business. This is personal. I look at
the cricket whites in my arms. When he stood in front
of me naked, I wanted to touch him, to run my hands
over his body, feel the hair on his torso, his softness,
his hardness, his arms around me, his body on top
of me. There was a voice inside me that wanted to
stop accusing him, tried to persuade me that the man
had done nothing wrong, the man who was standing in front of me naked, defenceless. That there was
probably a very good reason why he hadn't come
home last night. Why there was the smell of another
woman's perfume on his body. And that all he wanted
was for me to touch him too. But that split second
passed. I shake my head. And it is good that it passed.
Women forgiving their treacherous men. Treacherous middle-aged men. How fascinating. Nothing has
really changed. We might earn our own money, run
a company, share the childcare and the household
chores with our husbands, but when it comes down
to the basics, the most fundamental thing – sex –
nothing, absolutely nothing has changed. He goes out
to prove himself, like a testosterone driven monkey,
and she is willing to forgive him. Why? I get up and

the clothes drop from my lap on to the floor. I stand in front of the mirror. Because I too am middle-aged and no longer twenty? I take off my T-shirt and my bra. I let my skirt drop to the floor and take off my pants. Because I haven't shown my naked body to any other man for over a quarter of a century? I turn to the side. I have a good figure. Slightly more rounded than twenty years ago. And there is a tiny belly. But not much. No, it's not my body. I put my pants back on. When I look at my naked body, I feel happy with it. When I look at myself dressed I feel happy about it.

Of course, when we lie in bed I rarely feel a desire to make love to him. But that is not because of my body, or his body; it is because of my head. It's sometimes difficult to get my head around it. I can't switch my mind off. But that's always been the case. We've always gone through phases when we made either more or less love. This idea of regularly having sex x-number of times a week, ideally on the same days, never seemed to work for us. And it never bothered us. I put on my bra again. Should I feel guilty? Blame myself for my husband's lack of self-control? For his middle-aged man's fear of death, which he then tries to forget in the arms of a younger woman? I pull up my skirt. What am I supposed to do? Go down on my

knees, fling my arms around his legs, cry and beg him
not to leave me for a younger woman? And say that I
am so sorry and will promise to spread my legs every
evening? Anything to keep him . . .

I walk back into the study. Ridiculous. My thoughts
are ridiculous. My behaviour is ridiculous. Jim is ridiculous. And I won't run after him. I pick up the whites,
carry them back into the bedroom and leave them on
the bed. I could, of course, wait and see if he comes
back and asks for my forgiveness. Crawls back under
Mama's warm wings. We had a contract. An implicit
contract that related to trust and sexual loyalty. At least
that was my assumption. He has broken that contract.
And if there is one thing I have learned in business it is
that if people break a contract knowingly and wilfully
once, they will break it again. No need to be angry or
upset. It's human nature. I fetch the roll of black bin
liners from the kitchen drawer. Only I didn't have Jim
down as a contract breaker. And he probably wasn't.
But we are in a different phase of our lives now. New
phases bring different stresses. I walk back up the
stairs. But Jim's stress is his problem. At least now. If
he had come to me and said, Can we talk? But he didn't.
He acted his stress out and is probably still acting it
out.

I am back in the bedroom and rip one plastic bag off the roll. I open it. His children have now left home. And suddenly he sees a long empty road at the end of which lies death staring him straight in the face. He is lost. And scared out of his mind. I put the whites into the bag. Then I turn to the wardrobe. For a moment I hesitate. I could just sweep all these clothes into the bin liners in no particular order. But I don't yet know what I am going to do with the bags, so a systematic approach is more sensible. I pull the drawers with his pants out, followed by his socks. I lift the plastic bag. It's not too heavy yet and there is still plenty of room. I fit his T-shirts in too and close the bag with a knot. The next bin liner will contain his jumpers. I make sure that they remain folded, putting two piles next to each other at the bottom of the bag first. The anger has gone. The clearing out calms me. I keep focused on the task in hand, avoiding any thought of what it is exactly I am trying to achieve. I close the second bag and take the third, then drop it to the floor so as first to remove trousers and suits from the hangers and neatly fold them. I place the suit jackets flat on the bed, the front face down. I fold the sides and the sleeves over, ensuring that there aren't too many creases. I always felt lucky to have Jim as the father of my children. I carefully place a jacket on top of the clothes pile already in the bag. And I shouldn't denigrate our relationship. We have had many good times over the last twenty-five years. We share a similar sense of humour. We enjoy walking and hiking together. We talk well. He is intelligent, caring, good-looking. But. I have knotted the third bag. For a moment I stand still.

The three bulging big plastic sacks are leaning into each other. They might rip when I carry them down the stairs. I should put each one into another bin liner. I pick up the roll, rip the next bag off and then another two. I manage to stuff each full bag into another empty one. Yes, that's better. Though I should nevertheless hold them from underneath while carrying them downstairs. I look at the empty wardrobe. His shoes on the bottom shelf still need to go. I open another liner. I should use a double bag straight away. It's not easy pulling a second bag over a full one. I might have been able to deal with Jim's reluctance even to con-template having Mum move in. He has a point, as I have in fact admitted before. I have always found it difficult to be around Mum and I understood – and even shared – his fear that living together would not be a smooth ride. Even though she now needs our help, I could have excused and respected his point of view.

But this immature, crude way of asserting his independence by going and fucking the first woman who comes his way is unacceptable, hurtful and degrading. End of discussion. Four bags. I carry them downstairs, line them up in the hallway. I fill the plastic bowl from the kitchen sink with water and wipe the shelves and empty drawers. There is a surprising amount of dust. I close the doors.

'Stephanie, it's Michele. Jim and I discussed the basement conversion. We think it's a brilliant idea and would like to go ahead with it as soon as possible. Please call me when you get this message.'

I watch my hand lowering the phone on to the table and hear Helen from next door laughing in the garden. I turn my head. Through the open door I spot a white sock on the balcony. It must have fallen out from among the cricket whites.

3

CLARA CASTS A quick glance at the kitchen clock. Twenty-five minutes to eleven. Michele is always late. They are not going to make it to the osteopath in time. She gets up from the chair, unbuttons her coat and takes off her little hat – a light-blue pillbox hat matching the light blue of her coat. Even in summer she would never leave the house without hat and coat. Since half past nine she's been waiting for her daughter. In the hallway she places the hat on the table. For a moment she stands there patting it. When Hilary mentioned that Michele was going to pick her up, Clara knew it was a bad idea. Hilary is far more reliable than Michele. The old woman walks upstairs. She stops at the top and wonders why she came here. Yes, she remembers. She is looking for the clay model of the mother and child she made a few years ago. It's Michele's birthday in a couple of weeks, her forty-ninth, the last one before she is truly middle-aged. In the bedroom she opens the wardrobe. She'd love to

give her eldest daughter something special. Clara is staring at Edward's suits hanging there neatly. They were never that orderly when he was still with her. He was such a messy man. She spent her life clearing up behind him and the children. She bends down to reach the back of the shelf beneath the suits. She sighs. Her knees hurt. When the children were small she used to hide birthday and Christmas presents here. She feels along the shelf. Nothing – except dust. Bringing her dirty hand close to her face, she smells the dryness. Disgusting. Michele had recently sent a number of young women to look after the house. And what did they do? Clara's filthy hand proves yet again how right she was in showing these women the door. She closes the wardrobe. Surely she hasn't given the clay model away. She heads back downstairs to the kitchen. Quarter to eleven. Unbelievable. Michele is perfectly capable of being on time. But she picks and chooses. If it is in her interest, she is punctual. In fact she is just like Edward. In anything to do with his work, he was organized and conscientious. But at home, of course, he had a servant – his wife. Clara sits down again at the table. It is covered with pieces of clay. Ever since Edward's death she has enjoyed the freedom of not having to clear away her art at meal-

times. She herself doesn't care much for food anyway.
Never has. Some buttered toast and a bit of fruit will
do fine. Cooking and meals she provided for others
because they wanted them. Now finally she can con-
centrate on her work. She takes off her coat and lets
it fall over the back of the chair. Being irritated with
Michele brings on hot flushes. At the sink she retrieves
a dirty glass from beneath the unwashed plates. She
rinses it, fills it with water and drinks. Over the past
couple of days, ever since Hilary visited her last, she
hasn't had time to wash up. She is working on a vase
and thinking about it seems to take all her attention.
Time simply flies. It didn't use to.

As a girl she couldn't wait to grow up, especially
since they arrived in England just before the war
broke out. Her father, her British father, who had
married a German woman, her mother, in 1933,
because he believed he should support the Nazi
struggle against Communism, had finally realized
that saving the world from Communism wasn't the
Nazis' only aim, and that his native Norfolk might
after all be a better place for him and his family. They
moved into a dingy bedsit in Norwich. Five-year-old
Clara was spat at in school because her father had
never taught her proper English and she couldn't

hide her German accent. She hated going to school, but hated even more returning to that dingy bedsit where her mother hid all day in bed because she couldn't speak a word of English and was worried sick about her family back home. Time stood still in that bedsit and only sometimes crawled forward slowly, on all fours, when Father returned from work with a jar of jam and occasionally some sweets. And then suddenly, Clara can't remember when the transition happened, probably when she married Edward, time started to fly. And ever since, she hasn't been able to control it.

But back to the two clay figures of the mother and child. When Ruth from next door died a few months ago and the new people moved in, Clara panicked and worried that the new neighbours might break into her house at night. She invited them round once, a young professional couple, and they drank tea in her house. They were very interested in her work, especially the mother and child model, and the young woman – what was her name again? She can't remember. Anyway, as she was stroking the statue, the young woman mentioned that they were hoping to have a baby soon. Afterwards Clara decided to hide the piece. One can't be too careful. That's right. She hid it. But where? It must have been somewhere down here. She opens the cupboard under the sink.

'Hello, Mum. It's me,' Michele calls, pushing the door to her mother's house open. 'Mum?' she calls again as the door closes behind her. A clattering noise is coming from the kitchen.

Clara's head and shoulders have disappeared under the sink. A mouse shoots out of the cupboard and runs across the floor to the other side of the room, where it vanishes behind the dresser.

'What are you looking for?' Michele enquires matter-of-factly, while Clara continues to rummage in the cupboard. The mouse clearly didn't upset her. If she noticed it at all.

'I am looking for the clay model of the mother and child I made a few years ago. You know the one. Everyone said I should exhibit it.'

Michele turns on her heel and walks into the dark front room. Her mother never opens the curtains here, fearing that the neighbours will see her artworks. The smell of dust takes Michele's breath away. She grabs the model from the bookshelf.

'Here you go.' She places it on the draining board.

Clara has reappeared from beneath the sink and

straightens up – her knees might be in pain, but she is remarkably agile considering her frail frame and the fact that she only leaves the house when one of her daughters takes her out.

'Where did you find them? I was so worried that I'd lost them.' She looks at the two clay figures with great tenderness.

'They were where they've always been for the last thirty years.'

This clay model is her mother's best piece. She made it right at the beginning, when she started her pottery classes, around the time Michele and Hilary left home. She never produced anything of that quality again, concentrating rather on bowls, plates and jugs, giving them to her children as Christmas and birthday presents. Michele has a big box of them in the basement.

'They can't have been,' Clara contradicts her daughter sharply. 'I hid them a few months ago because of the new neighbours.'

Michele shakes her head but keeps quiet. There is no point arguing with her mother. She drops her bag on a chair and takes off her cardigan.

Clara looks at her daughter in surprise.

'I thought we were going to the osteopath. And you are terribly late.'

[24]

'Didn't Hilary call you? The osteopath cancelled the appointment half an hour ago. They had a water leak and Health and Safety insists that they need to sort it first. They were very apologetic. Hilary rebooked for next Wednesday when she will be able to take you.'

Michele walks over to the sink.

'She didn't call,' Clara says. 'I've been waiting since nine o'clock.'

Michele's hands glide into the yellow rubber gloves. When she is with her mother she feels as if she is underwater, holding her breath, hovering just beneath the surface, looking up. She can see and hear everything, but doesn't react or interact. She tries to hold her breath for as long as possible, waiting for the moment when she can resurface without danger of being attacked. She has learned to ignore most of her mother's comments. They often sound like accusations, but Michele isn't sure that her mother really means to accuse. It's simply her way of expressing her constant disappointment with the world. If she lets her mother's comments pass, Clara usually changes the subject quickly.

'What a lovely piece of work,' Clara now says. 'You know Ruth from next door, who died last year? Do you remember her? She got me into pottery in the first place. Do you remember? She did it for years. And someone had dropped out from their course and so she asked me, because she knew I was interested in art and did a bit of painting. Do you remember? No, you probably don't. Anyway, I made these lovely figures after three months. Three months. And Ruth attended classes for years and never produced anything of a similar standard.'

Clara walks over to the table.

'It's a pity really that Ruth and I didn't get on.'

Michele piles up the dirty dishes on the draining board. She has heard these stories before. She lets water run into the washing-up bowl.

'Are you rinsing with hot water?' Michele hears her mother say.

'Yes, I am, Mum.'

'Good. Because I will be able to smell the soap if you haven't.'

'Yes, I know you will, Mum.'

Michele has finished with the dishes. She wipes the worktop.

'By the way, you've got mice,' she says.

'I've never seen one,' Clara contradicts her daughter straight away.

'Well, I'm afraid you've got them.'

Michele presses down hard on an old egg-yolk stain that refuses to come off the Formica. Eventually she decides to scrape it away with a knife.

'I know why you make that accusation,' her mother suddenly says in an aggressive tone.

Michele straightens up, blowing a wisp of hair that has come loose from her ponytail out of her face. She places the knife in the washing-up bowl, wipes the food remnants off the surface and throws them into the bin next to the sink.

'Did you hear what I said?' her mother asks. 'Or do you now have the same hearing problem as your father?'

Michele rinses the cloth and hangs it over the tap. She places the gloves over the edge of the sink. This is going to be a difficult conversation, and she wanted to wait till she had taken her mother out for lunch. A restaurant seemed a safer place for this talk than here in the kitchen. But since Clara has now started, Michele knows her mother will not let go. So they might as well talk now.

'Would you like a cup of tea?' Michele asks, and puts on the kettle.

'Is that what you do when you negotiate your deals, offer tea?'

Michele turns off the kettle. She pulls a chair close to her mother, their knees nearly touching.

'Mum, we need to talk.'

'I am not going into an old people's home.' Clara leans back in the chair and folds her arms in front of her chest. Her blouse is covered in tea stains.

'How do you know that that's what I want to talk to you about?'

'Hilary told me last week that if it were up to you you'd put me away. Into storage. Lock me up, basically.'

'I don't think that's what Hilary said.' Michele's voice is calm. She manages to control her sudden anger with her sister. She hadn't expected Hilary to have mentioned to their mother the place that has become available at the residential home.

Clara looks down at her crossed arms like a sullen little child.

'Well, she told me you want to put me in an old people's home. Hilary doesn't like the idea either. And I certainly won't go.'

'You need help with the housework, and some regular company would be good for you too.'

'You can find some help for me,' Clara immediately agrees, her voice less panicky.

'You've had five nice, competent women in the last six months. You didn't like any and got rid of them all within a couple of weeks.'

'Your secretary chose them. She doesn't have a clue what I need.'

'Hilary and I personally interviewed the last two.'

'They were useless.'

Michele leans forward. She places both hands on her mother's crossed arms. But before she has time to respond, her mother says, 'Could you please move over to the other side of the table? I don't like you sitting so close to me.'

Michele takes her hands off her mother's arms and moves the chair a couple of metres along the round table. Then, deciding to make that cup of tea after all, she gets up and puts the kettle back on.

For a few seconds Clara stares at her eldest daughter's back, then she looks at the lump of clay she has picked up. She digs both thumbs deep into the mass, squeezing it outward into her palms. Michele is as cold as a fish. She can't get through to the girl. Never could. When Michele was very young, she used to wake up every morning at four and wouldn't go back to sleep. She wanted to play. Clara sat on the carpet with a cup of coffee and watched her daughter play. She'd ask, 'Why don't you sleep?' But Michele would just insist, 'Mama, play with me.'

Clara's hands press the clay into a flat shape. And now Michele wants to put her into storage, like an old piece of furniture. Clara flattens the shape on the table until it becomes as thin as a skin. Of course living on her own has been a struggle since Edward died. Although he was as deaf as a post for most of his life, he kept her company.

Hilary sat here on Wednesday, crying, 'I'd love you to come and live with me. But our house is far too small and I have the two boys.' Then she said that the only other option she could think of was living with Michele.

Clara shook her head. 'No, Hilary, that wouldn't work. Michele is always so busy. I would only be in the way.'

'She could convert the basement into a separate flat. There is enough space for a built-in wardrobe, so you could take Dad's clothes with you. You'd be living closer and it'd be less of an effort for me to see you. I would be much happier knowing you were living with

Michele rather than in an anonymous retirement home.'

Clara has had a few days to think about Hilary's suggestion. And the idea, far from perfect, has grown on her. Hilary would be happy and she could take Edward's clothes with her. The thought of throwing them out is unbearable. Whenever she wonders about it, the same picture comes into her head: she is climbing a big rubbish heap, smoke smouldering, rats chasing about beneath her feet, the reek sickening. She carries two black bin liners. At the top of the heap she stops and empties the bags. Edward's body is falling out. No, she won't ever throw her husband on to a rubbish heap.

She peels the clay skin off the table and kneads it back into a big lump.

'If you convert your basement, I'll happily come and live with you. But I know that you don't want me. And Jim doesn't like me,' Clara says. Michele pours the boiling water into the teapot.

When her sister suggested the basement conversion, Michele shook her head. 'I don't want Mum to move in with us. It's not a good idea. And besides, I work late at night and travel a lot.' She asked Hilary not to mention the basement to their mother. She didn't want to sow seeds of false hope. 'The residential home in Hampstead is ideal,' she said to her sister. 'It only takes fifteen residents at a time. It's close to us both. And Mum knows the area from when Dad and her lived there as a young couple. We are so lucky that a place has become available and even luckier that with the sale of Mum's house we will be able to afford it.'

'There won't be anything left for our inheritance after that,' Hilary objected quietly.

'Probably not. But we always knew it, didn't we?' For a moment Michele was astonished that Hilary was concerned about their inheritance. She never thought about it herself. 'And fortunately, neither of us is living on the breadline,' she concluded calmly.

Clara pulls one of the cups towards her. She lifts it to her lips and takes a few sips. She lowers it into her lap, holding on to it with both hands. Her eyes fill with tears. Michele's gaze is fixed on the cup in her mother's lap. It shakes; liquid drips on to Clara's skirt. Michele rises to her feet and removes the cup. Clara is now crying bitterly.

'I don't want to go into an old people's home,' she sobs.

Michele stands next to her mother's chair. One of her earliest childhood memories is of holding on to her mother's knee and looking up at a crying woman sitting at the kitchen table. She doesn't know how old she was. The image in her head is that of a two-year-old toddler. But she was probably older, because she vividly remembers the feeling of wanting to make it better for her mother. She ran off and returned with her favourite doll and placed it in her mother's lap, waiting for her to acknowledge the gesture. But her mother didn't notice. She just sat there and continued crying, sometimes muttering, 'I can't cope. I don't know what to do.'

'What can't you cope with? What can't you do?' Michele grew up haunted by these questions. For years she tried to help; for years she tried to make things better. But when she was a small child her mother would shoo her away, saying, 'Leave me alone. Give me some space.' And when Michele was older, these sentences turned into criticism: 'Can't you play on your own? Why can't you play on your own?' Until, as a teenager, Michele realized she couldn't make anything better for her mother. No one could make anything better for her mother. And she needed to escape the house otherwise she too might end up like Clara, sitting at a kitchen table, crying her eyes out because her mother never acknowledged the beautiful doll Michele had placed in her lap. Her favourite doll, her dearest possession, the one she hugged at night and whose hair she would twirl to help her fall asleep.

Michele kneels down and puts her arms around her mother. Clara feels tiny and very thin. She strokes her mother's back.

'Let's go for a walk along the river. It's beautiful weather outside. The fresh air will do us both good.'

4

CLARA – SIX MONTHS LATER

IT SMELLS OF fresh paint. It's disgusting. It gives me
a headache. I don't like the smooth walls. I don't like
sitting underground. Why have they thrown me out of
my house? They say I don't need such a big house any
longer. They say I have problems looking after myself.
Just because I fell down the stairs. I slipped. And then
I lay there. And I didn't want to get up. I was upset with
Michele. She wanted to put me into an old people's
home. Lock me up, put me into storage. I didn't like
Hilary's suggestion of moving in with Michele. And I
didn't know what to do. I wanted to stay in my own
house. But they say I can't look after myself any longer.
I can't look after the house any longer. That is non-
sense. I am not the tidiest. I am not the cleanest. But
everyone has to eat a bit of dirt before they die. I felt
safe in my house. Here I don't feel safe. The walls are
too white. Like in a madhouse. Michele never liked me.

I know. And Hilary told her to convert the basement. So she did. And now here I am, sitting in this basement. The walls are too white. And Edward's clothes are in a new wardrobe and I don't like the wardrobe at all. It's a built-in wardrobe. I never liked built-in wardrobes. His clothes don't belong there.

I sit in my rocking chair day in, day out. I rock back and forth, back and forth. I look at my clay on the big table. She bought me a big table too. Eventually. Hilary insisted. I put all the clay together in a big, round lump. It is sitting in the middle of the table, where it is drying out. I can't work surrounded by white walls and a strong smell of paint with a new table. I've been sitting in the rocking chair ever since I had to move in here. Michele is away all day and often at night too. I haven't seen Jim at all. They must have split up. She hasn't mentioned it or him. She doesn't talk to me about their relationship. Hilary comes once a day. She at least is happy. She loves how clean everything is here. She told me that they have put the house up for sale. My house in Rose Gardens. It's a lovely house. I don't know why I had to leave. One day they came and simply told me to leave.

Mum, you can't stay here any longer, they said. Both of them. Michele and Hilary. I fell down the stairs, that's true. And I didn't get up all night. I was upset. That's why I didn't get up. I think I could have got up. But I didn't. I wanted someone to come and help me. That's what I wanted. And when no one came, I started knocking on the wall. And then they came and took me to the hospital. And all I wanted was for Hilary and Michele to bring me home. But Hilary is always so concerned and Michele is not concerned enough. And so Hilary took me to hers and Michele simply agreed to Hilary's suggestion to convert the basement. Because Hilary nags and didn't want to drive across London. I never asked her to drive across London. I was happy in Rose Gardens. My children grew up there. I lived there with Edward. I did my pottery there. I never agreed to move out, but I wanted to please Hilary. I don't like the smell of new. It gives me a headache, and the pain and the smell blur my mind. I look at this lump of clay all day. I know if only I were to touch it, I could shape it into a beautiful artwork. No, I don't shape it. My hands would be guided by it. It would tell me its form and shape. I've been stuck far too long on vases and bowls, while all the time I knew I had it in me to create art. If only I were back home in my kitchen, where I always wanted to make art. First it was the children, then Edward and now again it is the children who are preventing me. Who put me into this white, soulless room. Hilary comes and takes me out. I go with her. Again to please her. I can't disappoint her. She needs someone to talk to. She's unhappy, has put on weight. Her boys are sweet but they run riot. Charles is no use. I wish she had a hobby, a passion. She claims she has no time. I tell her to cut her time with me short. I don't need company every day. Perhaps no company would do me good. I could let my mind drift. I would probably become calm and be able to approach the clay. It's a huge ugly piece. I have touched it. Sometimes I make it very smooth, like a giant ostrich egg. And then, a day or so later, I become angry and dig my nails into it. I don't destroy the egg shape, only the surface.

I jump up from my rocking chair. I hear it rocking back and forth, back and forth, click-clack, click-clack, behind my back as I am heading to the kitchen area, where I pull open the drawers, searching for a rolling pin or a steak hammer. But no! They took everything away from me. The drawers are almost empty. They say I don't need a rolling pin or a steak hammer or a garlic press or a cheese grater or a potato masher any longer. They say I never liked cooking anyway. There is a little cutlery in the drawers. Two knives, two forks, two soup spoons, two dessert spoons, two

teaspoons and a wooden spoon. They say I can't cook.
So are they expecting me to serve dinner for two?
Pathetic. I am so angry, I pull out all the drawers. I
enjoy the noise they make as they hit the floor. For
a moment I stand still and stare at the clutter on the
floor. I spot one knife close to my feet, the other over
by the cooker. I want a knife. I look around. There
are only these two pathetic table knives. They haven't
even given me a kitchen knife. Of course I could go
upstairs into Michele's kitchen. But I don't want to.
She is so particular. I am sure she knows exactly
how the cutlery is laid out in the drawer. And God
forbid I should disturb that order. No, I'd rather not.
Bending down is not the issue. I worry about rising
to my feet. Ever since falling down the stairs I can't
get rid of the pain in my right knee. Nothing bad. I'm
simply no longer as agile as I used to be. But I want
that knife. I lower myself down slowly, stretching my
bad leg towards the back so I don't need to bend it.
I am holding on to the worktop. It's a balancing act.
I shouldn't go all the way down, only far enough to
grab the knife. Nearly there. The fingertips of my free
hand are touching the cold metal. I lose my balance
and tumble forward. I land on the floor surprisingly
softly. I roll on to my side, lie motionless. I feel the

knife in my left fist. I close my eyes. But I open them straight away again. It's dangerous to close my eyes. I lose track of time. I shift closer to the worktop and pull myself up. Luckily my body is light. I manage. I knew I would. I could have pulled myself up from the bottom of the stairs too. But I didn't. I didn't want to. I wanted help. An old woman can't simply be left on her own.

Back at the table I stand and stare at the mass of clay. I slowly lower the knife and insert it into the soft lump. I turn it around a few times, then pull it out, lift the hand with the knife above my head and bring it back down with as much force as possible. A steak hammer would be better. I pull the knife out of the clay again, stab it, pull, stab, pull, stab. With my left hand I hold on to the edge of the table. I hear the knife hit the tabletop. Poor tabletop. It will be ruined. But I never liked the table. Eventually I am exhausted. The lump of clay has lost all its shape. I leave the knife stuck in it. Then I sit down in my rocking chair. They have put me into a cellar. Out of sight, out of mind. I won't have it.

5

MICHELE CAN HEAR the birds outside. The grey light of a breaking dawn is creeping through the blinds. She looks towards the alarm clock. Half past four. Her head is hurting. She gets up and puts on her dressing gown. In the kitchen she swallows two Nurofen. They didn't make love last night. By the time they returned home from the dinner party they were both too tired. The birds outside are by now wide awake and very noisy. Michele can still feel the alcohol in her system. She had a glass of champagne to start with, followed by a couple of glasses of wine. She knows she shouldn't mix alcohol, even sparkling and red. It will probably take all day for her body to deal with it. She fills a glass of water. Its tastelessness instantaneously makes her feel sick.

She climbs the stairs to the top floor. Theo's room resembles an empty shell, long since evacuated. Not even a child ghost lingers here any longer. She is now working for an advertizing firm in New York. Michele walks around the bed and opens the cupboard. When Thea visited over Easter, Michele asked her to sort out anything she no longer wanted. The rest they stored in the attic. Michele runs her hand along the empty hangers. She wants to redecorate the room. Thea can use it when she comes home, but it can also serve as a general guestroom. The only personal touches left are some postcards still stuck to the wall above the desk. Michele removes them, scraping off the Blu-Tack with her fingernail. She should call the decorators next week.

Felix's room still appears far more inhabited. He left for university two years ago and comes back most holidays. This summer, though, he's working in a bar in Brighton. It will be another couple of years at least before he moves out for good.

'Watch it, Michele. He might not move out at all,' Hilary likes to tease her sister. 'You've been incredibly lucky with Thea. She's an independent girl. Always has been. She's ambitious, like you. Felix, on the other hand, seems to go more for comfort. Like most young men nowadays. He'll crawl back into the warm nest once he's finished university.'

Michele sits down at his drum kit. She picks up two drumsticks, pretending to play. But suddenly she worries that she might hit them by mistake and returns the sticks to their place. On the middle floor she opens the balcony door in the study. A cool breeze enters the room. This is Jim's and her favourite room in the house. Ceiling-high bookshelves fill every inch of wall space. She sits down in one of the two big old armchairs in the middle of the room. She puts her feet up on the coffee table. They sit here to read books, to listen to music or to make love on the Persian rug in front of the roaring fire in winter, or in the dark in front of the open balcony doors in summer. The wind plays with the light curtains. She closes her eyes. She feels the hard floor beneath her back and feels Jim thrusting inside her. She hears herself laughing, pulling Jim's head down, asking him to be quieter. 'Shh, the children might hear us.' She sits on top of him and feels the fire on her naked body and his hands on her buttocks. But these are all images from years ago.

Michele slides into bed. Jim hasn't stirred. His breathing is deep and regular. She moves closer to his back. She puts an arm around him and places her hand on his chest and her nose against his neck.

~

The phone rings far away. They are in a grotty hotel, Jim, the children and her. The children are still young. The sheets on the beds are dirty. Michele wants to go and complain, but Jim says, 'I don't like it when you complain.' Then she hears the phone ring. She knows that it isn't her mobile. Nevertheless, she finds herself looking in her handbag. The phone keeps on ringing. It's becoming louder. Then it is quiet. She looks down the long hotel corridor. She feels someone tapping her shoulder.

'Michele? Darling.'

She senses Jim sitting down on the bed next to her. His hand is resting on her shoulder.

'I just had a dream,' she mumbles, pulling the duvet up to her chin. She wants to go back to the hotel to see what happens next. Why did they visit the hotel in the first place? And the children were so young. She has a feeling that they've been to this hotel before, have left something there and have now returned to fetch it. She needs to get back to her dream to figure out what she was supposed to find.

'Michele.' Jim shakes her shoulder gently again. 'Sorry to wake you, darling. But your sister is on the phone. She's distraught and refuses to go until you've spoken to her.'

Michele finally opens her eyes. For a moment she lies totally still. The dream has gone.

'What time is it?' she asks.

'Eight fifteen.'

She turns on her back and looks at Jim. He is fully dressed.

'I was just on my way out to get some croissants. It's a beautiful day.' He rises to his feet.

'I was thinking . . . we haven't been to an exhibitions for months. I also wondered about going to a matinee.'

He is already at the door. He stops for a moment and points to the study, whispering, 'Your sister . . . Don't forget.'

Michele is tempted to turn around, pull the duvet over her head and go back to sleep. She feels drowsy and heavy. But then she sits up, throws off the cover and jumps out of bed. She takes the phone from the desk in the study and sits down in the chair facing the open balcony door. Jim must have opened it. She rests her head against the back and looks up into the clear blue sky. They should go on holiday. Somewhere warm. As soon as the Sea Shelf 3 deal is finalized.

'Hi, Hil. It's me.'

'Thank God you are up . . .'

Hilary starts sobbing. Michele lifts her outstretched right foot and looks at her painted toenails.

'Mum is in hospital.'

Michele lets go of her foot and straightens her back.

'Why?'

Again sobbing.

'Hil, what happened?'

'She fell down the stairs.'

'Which stairs?'

'The big ones.' More sobbing. 'Apparently she tried to call . . . to call you. As she was lying at the bottom of the stairs.' Sobbing. 'She couldn't move. But the mobile was in her skirt pocket. And then she fell and then she tried to call you, but you didn't pick up . . .'

Michele stands up and walks out on to the balcony. The wooden decking feels cool under her bare feet. She forbids her mind to race ahead.

'Has she broken anything? Is she conscious?'

Michele pauses to give Hilary a chance to catch her breath. The panting becomes less audible. A pigeon settles on a branch in the pear tree, gently bobbing up and down in the wind.

Hilary's sobbing resumes.

'I can't do anything if you don't tell me the facts,' Michele says.

'The facts, the facts, the facts! You always want to know the damn stupid facts. I'll give you the facts: Mum needed our help last night and we weren't there. She was at the bottom of the stairs all night, knocking on the neighbours' wall. Tap, tap. Tap, tap. All night long. Until they finally woke up and wondered about the noise and knocked on her door. Then they called the police, who broke the door down.'

The pigeon looks incredibly happy and content on its branch. It is quite amazing how such a thin branch can support such a fat pigeon.

'Why didn't she call an ambulance if she had the phone in her hand?'

'I don't know!' Hilary screams hysterically. 'How should I know? Perhaps her battery was flat.'

Michele realizes that this was the wrong question to ask.

'Has Mum broken anything, Hilary? Is she conscious?' Michele repeats, her voice now stern.

'She is so confused. And so frightened.'

'What does the doctor say?'

A vision of their mother in a hospital bed, unable to move, has appeared in Michele's mind.

'I haven't spoken to any doctor. Mum called. We need to go and pick her up.'

Michele interrupts her sister. 'Which hospital?'

'They say she's fine. Didn't you hear what I said?' Hilary is beside herself. 'They won't tell you anything different. She is fine. But she isn't. And she won't ever be. Do you understand? And it's our fault. I promised Dad we'd look after Mum.'

'Hilary, I am sorry but I'm not going to talk to you any further until I've spoken to the hospital myself.'

The pigeon suddenly opens its wings and flies away. The branch continues to bob. There is a silence at the other end of the phone. Michele fixes her gaze on the bobbing branch. It anchors her.

'What's the name of the hospital?'

'Chelsea and Westminster.'

'Which ward?'

'I don't know. And there is no point ringing them. You won't be able to speak to anyone there. We need to go.'

'We will go. I will get dressed and pick you up.'

Michele cuts the line before her sister has time to say anything else. She steps from the balcony inside.

For a moment she stands motionless at the desk, gathering her thoughts. Then she sits down, wakes the computer out of sleep mode and Googles the hospital to check the phone number. The hospital confirms that her mother was admitted, but no doctor is available to talk to Michele.

6

MICHELE – NINE MONTHS LATER

I HEAR THE noise of the Hoover coming around the corner. My office door is open. I've been staring at the screen for over an hour, senselessly clicking on sites to waste my time. At least if I had bought a dress, a suit, some shoes. We need new towels, too. But I haven't. I couldn't make up my mind. If I can't tear myself away from my desk, I should at least have gone through my emails, trying to reduce my ridiculously full inbox. But I haven't done that either. I am mentally exhausted. It's easier to stay glued to the computer than to focus my mind and my body on leaving. The cleaner has come around the corner. She is waving at me. I wave back with a smile. We have seen each other before. Numerous times. Although she is employed by a cleaning company, she's probably been coming here for two, perhaps even three years. Anita from Portugal. She continues to hoover. I stare at the screen once more and can't even make up my mind whether to buy some shoes. I don't want to go home.

Anita has stopped hoovering and is wiping down the lift doors. I pretend to be busy at my screen. I click on the John Lewis site. I could at least order some towels. Most of our towels are a disgrace, worn so thin that they have holes and are frayed at the edges. I see the dark-blue and dark-green towels my mother-in-law gave us as a wedding present. I never liked them. I don't want a dark colour. But I don't want white or pink or light blue either. Hil has nice towels. Cath Kidston, that's it. That's where they're from. I scroll down the towel list to see if they do Cath Kidston. I could buy a couple for Mum, too.

I've done the right thing with Mum moving in. The conversion worked well and they were incredibly quick. Twelve weeks from start to finish. We've moved her furniture and most of her stuff. We went through it with her to see what she wanted to take. Her main concerns were her pottery and Dad's clothes. I decided that we should take all the books. I had asked the builder to put shelves along the free walls. Nearly all my parents' books found a space. We also took the paintings. Hilary visits her every morning and I found Larissa, who comes between four and seven. I am happy with Larissa. Sarah recommended her, so she must be good.

The Cath Kidston towels on the John Lewis site have sold out. I google Cath Kidston and click on the link. Beautiful towels with lovely patterns in light colours. I order five small towels and five bath towels. Then I add two small and two big ones for Mum.

I don't like to think of her sitting in our converted basement. I'm rarely home. I often work late. Mum doesn't sleep much. She is always awake when I get home. And she hears me coming in, although the basement is practically a self-contained flat. But we kept the door to downstairs. In case Mum needs help quickly. And this door is always open. Mum asked for it. And of course I understand. I wouldn't want to be locked away in a cellar either.

'Michele, darling, is that you?' I hear her call the moment I unlock the front door. I then feel obliged to go down and say hello and we sit together. She in her rocking chair, click-clack, click-clack, backwards and forwards. I usually make tea and sit with the cup on my lap at her kitchen table. It was easier when she was still living in her own house. Whenever I visited her, I busied myself with something – washing the dishes, washing her clothes. Now everything is already done by Larissa. And even when I go back upstairs, it's never as if I am closing the door. I can only close the door to my bedroom now. Therefore, at the weekend, if I am at home, I tend to sleep late and then read for hours in bed. I have started to take a Thermos with me to my room in the evening. I have lukewarm coffee in the morning and can avoid going down to the kitchen. I like Mum to believe I sleep until two or three in the afternoon.

'You are like a teenager,' she said last Sunday.

She doesn't of course know how right she is. She was merely referring to my weekend sleeping habits.

'Mrs Michele is working late these days.'

I am startled and lift my eyes. Anita is standing in the door. I take off my reading glasses.

'You are working late too,' I say, smiling.

'But my work day doesn't start until six in the evening.'

For a moment we smile at each other in silence. I need to change the subject.

'How is your son?'

Her son is twenty-five and has broken his leg. He is living at home again after a brief marriage. He wants to look for a job but hasn't because of his broken leg.

Apparently the fracture is not healing properly. The doctor messed up. I make the appropriate noises: 'Oh, poor him!' 'Oh, poor you!' I put my glasses back on as a sign that I need to return to my work. Just as she is about to turn away, I remember the fridge.

'Anita, could you please clean the fridge today? Thank you.'

'It's on my list of things to do, don't you worry, Mrs Michele.'

I fetch my purse from my handbag, type in my card number and pay for the towels. For a moment I hesitate, then I click on the Chie Mihara shoe site. I know their new spring/summer collection by heart. I am on this site almost every night. I have now finally made up my mind to buy a pair. After all, I am already holding the card in my hands. I order high-heeled green sandals. They will go beautifully with my red summer dress.

7

CLARA LIES IN a room with eight beds. The nurse who greeted the sisters said that she would be able to leave in the next couple of hours.

The rubber soles of Michele's flat canvas shoes squeak on the linoleum floor. Hilary hasn't said a word in the car on their way to the hospital.

'No scenes in front of Mum. We'll talk later.' Michele briefly touches Hilary's hand.

Clara's bed is the third on the right. A large, noisy family is gathered around the patient opposite. They speak Russian. Michele knows a few words from her business trips. A blanket covers Clara's body up to her chin. Her face is as pale as the wall behind her. Her eyes are wide open, staring at the ceiling. Michele kisses her mother on the forehead. Fright has turned Clara's eyes into two blank circles.

'Please get me out of here,' Clara whispers without taking her eyes off the ceiling.

Hilary has moved around to the other side and

places her head next to her mother's face on the pillow. Michele draws a chair closer to the bed. Underneath the blanket she feels for her mother's hand. It is ice cold.

'Are you freezing?' she asks.

Clara shakes her head. Then turns her face to look into Hilary's eyes, repeating, 'Please get me out of here.'

Hilary is fighting back tears. 'Yes, we will. We are waiting for the doctor to check you out and then we can take you home.'

'Good.' Clara closes her eyes. Her breathing becomes deeper.

Michele has moved her mother's hand from underneath the blanket, holding it now between her palms. For the moment her mind is still. But she knows that the situation has changed; decisions will have to be made far more quickly than she anticipated. Suddenly the curtains are drawn around them. Michele and Hilary both jump.

'We gave your mother a couple of sleeping pills just before you arrived,' the nurse explains. 'She didn't sleep all night. Why don't you grab a coffee outside and come back in an hour to take her home?'

∽

'You know what that means?' They are standing outside the building. Tears are streaming down Hilary's face. She throws her arm randomly up towards one of the floors. 'We can't leave Mum alone. We can't just simply drive her home and leave her there and pretend nothing has happened.'

Michele looks briefly into Hilary's anguished face, then her eyes wander across her sister's shoulder to the other side of the road. She thought she saw a café when they parked the car. Yes, there it is. She puts her hand on Hilary's arm.

'Let's have a coffee.'

Hilary doesn't move.

'I will take Mum home with me,' she says.

Michele stares again into Hilary's face. Left-over mascara from last night has smeared under her eyes, which are red from crying and lack of sleep.

'You don't have to play the martyr.'

She gently wipes the mascara from Hilary's face. Hilary throws her arms around Michele. For a moment they hug.

'Charles is fine with it. I've already mentioned it,' Hilary continues after they have sat down with their coffees at a small table on the pavement.

'And I spoke to Maria before I came to pick you up,' Michele says.

The coffee is doing Michele's lingering headache good. Hilary looks at her questioningly.

'The last woman we employed for Mum,' Michele explains. 'She offered to come back. She lives on the road parallel to Mum's. She needs the money. She is good and I trust her. She could even come tonight. On Wednesday we will look at the home in Hampstead. You'll see, it's beautiful. Perfect for Mum, perfect for us because it's so close.'

An ambulance with its siren on approaches and turns into the forecourt of the hospital. For a moment talking becomes impossible. Michele empties her coffee cup.

'Mum kicked her out once,' Hilary says. 'It's not a good start.'

'Maria wouldn't hold it against her.'

Another ambulance with its siren on pulls up. When the wailing stops, Hilary suggests they walk down to the river.

There are strong currents flowing beneath Battersea Bridge. In the distance the sun glints on the surface of the water. A beautiful white boat passes.

'I'll take Mum back with me, we'll look at the home on Wednesday and perhaps in the meantime you could ask your architect friend for a quote to convert the basement,' Hilary says.

A girl waves at them from the boat. The two women wave back.

'It is just so that we have an idea how much it would cost,' Hilary continues. 'It might be far too expensive. It might not be possible at all, because of building regulations or what have you. But then at least we'll know there's no alternative to the home.'

Michele puts both hands on the iron railings and wonders if she feels pushed into a corner by Hilary's suggestion. The wind blows her skirt gently against her legs. They could be at the seaside. Almost. Hilary is offering her a compromise. A very reasonable suggestion. If Hilary takes Mum for the next week or so, the least Michele can do is obtain a quote from Stephanie. She will, however, also call the residential home to enquire how long they have to decide. If need be, she is willing to pay for the first couple of months straight away so that the place is guaranteed. She won't of course tell Hilary or her mother. And she won't tell Jim about the quote for the basement conversion.

On Wednesday Hilary calls. Jack has fallen off the swings. He seems to be fine but she'd better take him to A&E for X-rays to make sure he hasn't hurt his head. Michele hears her eight-year-old nephew wailing in the background.

'I won't be able to visit the home today,' Hilary apologizes. 'I'm sure you understand.'

8

CLARA – TEN MONTHS LATER

I HEAR HER turn the key, open the door, close it. For a moment there is silence while she quietly removes her shoes. Then she tiptoes into the kitchen. I hear her take a glass. Silence. Then water is running out of the tap. I know she will stand at the top of the stairs to the basement, holding her breath, listening. Nothing except darkness will meet her. I am pretending to be asleep. But I am sitting in my chair, motionless. I stopped rocking when I heard the taxi outside. Only my toes touch the floor. The muscles in my legs are straining. I hope I don't get cramp. I wish I had put the soles of my feet down. Now I don't dare move, even slightly. I might lose control and the runners might hit the ground hard, too hard, and Michele might hear. I don't want her to know that I am still awake. I don't want her to come down.

9

MICHELE PLACES THE tip of the knife on to the ridge of the fish's back and slits it open.

'I spoke to Felix today,' Jim says.

She inserts the blade and slips it underneath the skin.

'Did you know he has a girlfriend?' Jim continues. 'He sounds happy.'

Michele places the fork behind the gills and pushes down to sever the head. She puts skin and head on her spare plate.

'He sent me a picture of them both.' Jim fetches his iPhone. 'A stunning blonde.'

He hands the phone to Michele. She wipes her hands on her napkin.

'She looks so in love with my little boy,' Michele coos at the small screen in her hands. 'What does she do?' she asks, handing the phone back to Jim.

'She's studying medicine at Edinburgh and is working in the same bar as Felix this summer. She loves hiking. They went to Wales last weekend, just the two of them with a tent. And she loves dogs.'

Jim has not bothered to dissect the fish as neatly as his wife. Instead he now digs straight into its body, while Michele smiles to herself. Felix has always loved dogs, in fact animals full stop. And his biggest regret so far in life has been that his mother never allowed him a dog as a child.

'Well, she appears to be the woman for him!' she says.

Jim is pulling a big bone out of his mouth, nodding. For a moment they eat in silence.

'I had a meeting with George today,' Michele says eventually. 'He still has his doubts about Sea Shelf 3. He doesn't trust Rashid, despite the new geology report.'

Jim's head is bowed low over his plate, sieving through the bones for some fish.

'Are you listening to me?' she asks after a brief pause. A cold chill touches her bare arms. Further south, down by the river, a thunderstorm must already be raging.

'Yes, I am,' he replies without lifting his eyes.

'But you don't want to talk about my work?'

'No, I don't want to talk about it.' He looks up. 'I would like to talk about something different.'

'Like what?'

He shrugs. 'How is your mother?'

'Fine.'

'Is she still staying with your sister?'

'Yes.'

'Have you spoken to the home, so they'll keep the place?'

'What do you think? Of course I have.' She pauses, then mumbles, 'Sorry.'

Goosebumps are spreading down her arms. She pushes her chair back and steps over the ledge of the garden door, catching the handle to pull the door shut. On the garden table she spots the mother-and-child clay model that her mother gave her last Saturday as an early birthday present.

'Why are the figures out there?' She fetches the model, turning to shut the door.

'Let's leave the door open. It'll rain in a moment and the smell will be wonderful.' Jim puts candles on the table.

'If we leave the door open, the wind will blow out the candles in no time,' Michele remarks.

'These tea lights will be fine,' Jim says, striking a match.

Michele places the clay model on to the worktop, then picks up the cardigan from the kitchen sofa. The wind will prove her right soon enough. As she lifts knife and fork again, thunder rumbles, but still far away. Michele watches the dancing flames.

'So why was the clay model out there?'

She pushes some fish on to the fork. Last Saturday after returning home from her mother's, she put the clay model on the mantelpiece in the living room. Her mother's gesture had touched her. She hadn't ever expected Clara to let go of her most precious artwork, and certainly not to give it to her eldest daughter.

'I wanted to put it in the basement with your mother's other stuff. But I must have got distracted.'

'Why?'

Michele examines the full fork lying on her plate. The white fish sits perfectly on it. No tiny bits are hanging over the edges.

'Why?' Jim repeats the question, as if he didn't understand it. 'Because it's hideous, darling. And so I thought that's where you would like it to go.'

He pours himself another glass of prosecco. Michele's is still full.

'My mother gave me this model as an early birthday present.' She lifts her eyes from her neatly packed fork. 'I like it.'

Jim's little finger disappears into his mouth,

removing food from between his teeth. A sudden gust of wind blows out all four candles.

'What did I tell you!' With a movement of her head, she points to the candles.

Jim takes his finger out of his mouth and relights them. The first raindrops are falling. Michele finally puts her full fork into her mouth. The fish by now is cold. She chews. It might as well be rubber. She washes the food down with a large gulp of alcohol.

'I'd like it to stay on the mantelpiece,' she says.

'I really don't like it, Michele. What is it supposed to be, anyway?'

'A mother and child.'

He laughs. 'A mother and child? Well, you need a lot of imagination to see that.'

'Which you obviously don't have.'

A thunderbolt rips through the air. Michele jumps.

'You see, even the gods agree with me,' she says, laughing.

'The gods may agree with you,' Jim comments drily. The shadows cast by the flames on her face make his wife look gaunt. 'But I don't. And it will certainly not stay on the mantelpiece in the living room. It's so awful and badly done . . .'

'Stop it! Don't talk like that about my mother.'

'I'm talking about the heap of clay – not your mother.'

Without warning, water starts gushing down from the heavens. The candles on the table blow out again. Both Jim and Michele turn their heads and stare at the rain in silence.

'Shall we make love in the rain?' Jim says finally, without looking at his wife.

Michele leans back in her chair, shaking her head. 'I can't believe you've just said that.'

Jim shifts, then calmly, with a deliberate movement, lights the candles once more.

The rain splashes hard on to the patio. He gets up, scrapes his half-eaten dinner into the bin and opens the dishwasher. Michele watches the candles blow out for the third time. She's been waiting for it to happen.

'I wish you would listen to me,' she snorts. 'As long as the door stays open, there is no point in lighting the candles.'

He closes the dishwasher. She takes a sip of her prosecco and puts the glass back on the table in the exact position where it stood before. Without another glance at his wife, Jim walks out of the kitchen. A moment later the front door slams. Michele doesn't move. Eventually she grabs her glass and empties it in one go. The wine tastes flat and sweet. The bubbles have gone and so too, it seems, the alcohol. She refills her glass and empties it. Her head finally starts to feel light. Her reflection in the glass door resembles a pale ghost with a shapeless mane of hair. She switches off all the lights, opens the doors to the garden wide. She drinks the last of the prosecco straight from the bottle. When she presses the speed-dial with Jim's number, his phone rings on the dresser, where he had placed it after showing Michele the picture of their son.

10

MICHELE – ELEVEN MONTHS LATER

I CLOSE MY bedroom door and place the glass of
water on the bedside table. I slide my computer
bag from my shoulder and drop it, together with my
handbag, on the old armchair. I place my shoes next to
each other underneath the chair. I take off my jacket,
blouse and skirt. I hang the hangers with the clothes
on the outside of the wardrobe door to air overnight.
I didn't make the bed this morning, nor did I draw
the curtains back. I sit down at the dressing table. It's
a beautiful Art Deco piece made out of cherry wood.
My right hand strokes the soft curve of the small
drawers. Only then do I glance briefly at myself in the
mirror. My face looks tired and naked. The make-up
has long since worn off. My hair needs a wash. I lift
my arms to remove the pins and my hair falls to my
shoulders. I search in my earring box and take out
the long ruby ones. I call them ruby, but in actual fact

they are cheap things from Accessorize, one of my many airport purchases. I hold them against my ears. They match the dark-red lace of my bra. I should go to bed. I shouldn't sit here playing at dressing up. But it helps me to unwind. I remove the little gold studs from my earlobes and put in the big earrings. I search through my lipsticks and pull out the bright red one. I very rarely wear it. It has an orange tint and complements my hair perfectly. But I always feel it adds too much colour to my face if you consider my bright blue eyes.

Jim laughs. 'A man sees your amazing eyes, your wonderful hair. I can't see that anything clashes.'

He stands behind me and leans forward to plant a kiss on my neck. I look at us in the mirror. He glances up and our eyes meet, while his hands gently cup my breasts.

'And your breasts are the best part of you.'

I wonder if I should wiggle to shake him off. We have to be at Tony and Mel's at eight and we are already running late. He is wearing his suit. I haven't even got beyond the lipstick yet. Then I lean back into him. I close my eyes, gently removing his hands from my body. I swing around on the stool and put my hands behind his neck before he has time to straighten up. We kiss. 'Melanie can wait for ten minutes,' I say. 'We're late as it is.' My lips on his, while I start to loosen his tie. Squeaking noise from the TV downstairs. We both smile at each other like naughty children. I stand up, go to the door and shut it. In the meantime Jim has sat down on the bed, undoing the laces of his shoes. I push him back on to the bed and climb on top of him. 'Let's not waste time with undressing.' I hear his shoes fall to the floor behind me.

In the mirror I see my right hand now move along the lace of my bra. I feel a vague longing between my legs.

'You use what?' My sister, quite drunk by now, lurches forward on to the table, roaring with laughter. I take another big sip from the whisky in my hand. My vision is already blurred. I've drunk so much this evening that I no longer feel the amber liquid go down my throat like fire. It's more like water now. I put down my glass, wiping away tears of laughter. How on earth did we get on to this subject? How on earth did I end up totally drunk in my sister's kitchen? I suddenly freeze. What day of the week is it? No, nothing to worry about. It's Friday.

'Why are you shaking your head?' My sister has sat up straight on the other side of the table.

I wave my hand in the air. 'I had a sudden panic, wondering what day of the week it was.'

'It's Friday, you silly. Would you be so carefree otherwise, and sit in my kitchen drinking? No way. So –' she pushes her glass across the table and knocks against mine – 'back to what you were saying.'

I decide to go to the loo first.

'Oh, the suspense,' Hil moans, rolling her eyes.

'You won't be disappointed,' I say over my shoulder, holding on to the frame of the kitchen door.

'No way!' my sister exclaims, as I place the electric toothbrush I have picked up from the bathroom in the middle of the table like a trophy. 'I thought I misheard.'

I sit down and empty my glass. Hilary inhales audibly and theatrically.

'You have hidden depths, big sis.'

Then she suddenly breaks out laughing again. 'What did you just do in the loo?'

I grab the bottle and pour myself some more. 'I only use a toothbrush with a pink ring.'

Hilary hits the table with the flat of her hand. I laugh, mightily pleased by my quick wit.

'Joking aside,' Hilary then says, trying to keep a straight face, 'why an electric toothbrush? You surely have money for some sexier device.'

'Pah, kinky toys. No thanks. This does the trick much better. Two minutes and you are done. And sometimes not even that long.'

I now keep one in the drawer of the dressing table. Which means I don't have to go to the bathroom to fetch the other one. I don't want to run the risk of Mum hearing my bedroom door opening, closing, opening, closing, and wondering what I am doing or calling out for me, leaving me feeling guilty. What I do in my bedroom is my own private affair. I open the drawer.

I feel the heat rising. I open my legs wider, put my feet up against the dressing table.

I never see Jim. Though I see a man. Anonymous. A man I paid with a young, firm body. I never see his face. I only feel him inside me. We are in a dark little back alley. Or in a small office storeroom.

My lower body convulses. My heart doubles its speed.

I'm always dressed. The man is sometimes dressed. And sometimes I see his naked torso. Feel it.

I turn the toothbrush off. Put it back into the drawer. I open my wardrobe and wonder what to wear tomorrow. Summer has arrived. Today the temperature climbed up to twenty-four degrees. I look through my summer dresses. None are suitable for the office. I pull them out, lay them on to the bed, then I try them on, one after the other, matching them with the new high-heeled green sandals. All of them still fit. I hadn't really expected anything else, but it is still good to know. By the time I've tidied the clothes away, it's twenty past one. I put the alarm on for four thirty. I have to catch a plane to Frankfurt at seven.

11

JIM RUNS DOWN the road, then slows and continues up the hill in a light jog. His shirt is soon soaked from the rain. If he'd been wearing trainers he'd be lighter on his feet. He has no idea where he is heading. He simply had to get out of the house. When he reaches Hampstead Lane, the rain has stopped. He speeds up. The yellow light from the street lamps reflects on the wet tarmac. His legs feel heavy but his breathing has become easier. A stitch in his side suddenly makes him bend over. He has nearly reached the Spaniards Inn; a small group of people are leaving the pub, laughing. He would love a beer. Straightening up, he searches in his trouser pockets for change. Nothing. Not a penny. Stupid to have left the house without his wallet. Without a jacket. At least he grabbed his keys. He carries on running towards Hampstead. Gus might be in. Worth a try. Jim and Gus have known each other since university. They both have a weak spot for heavy metal and have kept in touch by meeting once a year for a gig featuring one of their ailing heroes. Three months ago they saw Iron Maiden. For over twenty years Gus worked as a successful City lawyer and earned enough to retire five years ago. His marriage broke up soon afterwards. His wife, who was fifteen years his junior, wanted children, but he didn't. He now occupies the airy top part of an old Victorian house in the Vale of Health, takes guitar lessons and is planning to buy a vineyard in the South of France. Jim sees the light in Gus's flat as he approaches the house.

'Wow! Did she chuck you out?' Gus exclaims when he opens the door. 'You look like a drowned rat.'

'Long story,' Jim replies.

'I'll fetch you a dry shirt.'

'Thanks,' says Jim, who can feel the chill from his wet clothes on his skin now that he has stopped running.

As they are heading out of the door again fifteen minutes later, Jim asks, 'Can I borrow a hundred from you?'

'The night is on me.' Gus's hand comes down on Jim's shoulder. Then he pulls out a banknote. 'So that you are not entirely cashless.'

~

The pub Gus has recommended on Upper Street is crowded. A band is playing. The two men manoeuvre their way through to the bar. Just as they are about to head back out with their pints, Gus spots an empty table in the corner next to the small stage. He points to it, shouting above the noise, 'Our chance! Or would you prefer to go outside?'

Jim nods in the direction of the table. He doesn't feel like talking. Perhaps after a couple of pints. Gus will understand. He leans back against the wall, his mind empty, the loud bass filling his body. The glass becomes lighter in his hand. Gus nudges him. Jim opens one eye.

'Another one?'

Jim nods and closes his eyes again.

'Some very pretty women around,' he hears Gus say.

Jim smiles. He has had enough of women for the day. When he becomes aware of his second glass being nearly empty, he stands up. Gus nods in agreement to a third pint.

Waiting to be served at the bar, Jim scrutinizes the room. The average age is about twenty to thirty years younger than him. And a lot of young women. All looking very similar. And very good. Long blonde hair, long beautiful legs in miniskirts, very high heels.

He orders his two pints, takes one in each hand and, just as he is about to make his way back through the crowd, someone pushes against him from the side. He accidentally kicks the calf of the woman next to him. He hears her sharp intake of breath. Beer spills on to her arm. She is a head smaller than him. He looks down into her face, she looks up at him. He notices her shining bright eyes. A brief expression of indignation flickers across her face.

'I am so sorry,' he shouts above the noise.

She wipes the liquid off her naked arm, while her eyes don't let go of his face.

'Lucky I'm wearing short sleeves.' She smiles.

Jim can detect a slight foreign accent, but it is too loud to decipher where it is from. He smiles back at her. She is older than some of the others. Early to mid-thirties, he guesses.

'It's so crowded in here,' he says, lifting the glasses above his head as he feels another push from behind, forced to step closer to the woman. His body briefly touches hers; he can smell her flowery perfume. He quickly nods, then turns to head back to the table.

A few minutes later the band stops playing, announcing a half-hour break. Jim scans the room, conscious of who he is looking for. Gus follows his gaze.

'Attractive woman,' he says.

Jim furrows his brow. The bar is hidden behind two large pillars. Gus points to the big mirror on the wall behind them. Jim twists his neck. A clear view of the bar. The woman is talking to a female friend.

'They're regulars,' Gus now says. 'I've never seen them with any man.'

Jim drinks half his pint. The alcohol starts to wash away the tension from the early evening.

'Fancy a bite to eat?' he enquires. His half-eaten fish didn't leave him satisfied. And he needs some food in his stomach to absorb the alcohol. He puts the glass on the table. He catches a glimpse of two laughing women moving through the crowd. He looks in the direction they seem to be heading and sees two empty chairs at a table a few metres away.

'There is a lovely Indian down the road,' Gus replies.

The women are now sitting down. The one Jim spoke to smiles briefly in his direction but has already averted her eyes before he has time to reach

'Let's go,' he says.

He stands up, gulps down the rest of his beer. He lifts the black leather jacket he borrowed from Gus off the back of his chair. For a second it feels as if he is about to lose his balance, then he stands firmly rooted on the ground again.

'Shall we get some company for our dinner?' he asks, slightly surprised at his bold suggestion. But who cares? After all, he is a mature man in control of himself.

'You know me. I am not going to decline,' Gus answers.

Jim heads straight for the table with the two women.

'May I give you my telephone number?' He grins.

She looks up at him. If she is surprised she certainly doesn't show it.

'No, thank you,' she replies.

Her tone, however, is soft. Jim didn't expect her to say yes; in fact, he would have been disappointed if she had.

'What a pity. May I have your phone number?' he then asks without batting an eyelid.

She shakes her head. But her eyes shine brightly.

'It's not my lucky day, is it!'

She raises her eyebrows playfully, slowly shaking her head.

With a twinkle in his eye, he then says, 'Two more proposals. My friend and I could join you here for a drink, or you could join us for dinner at a restaurant of your choice on Upper Street.'

The women exchange a quick glance.

'We have no objections to your joining us at the table.' She pauses before adding, 'If you can find two chairs.'

She nods at the table behind him, the one Gus and Jim have just left. Jim looks over his shoulder. A couple are sitting down.

'Ladies, don't you worry. We will sort this out.'

Gus has now stepped in, gesturing theatrically, before forging his way through the crowd to the other side of the room. Jim catches up with him, just as Gus is about to lift two chairs.

'I'm not sure this is a good idea. I chatted them up; it was fun. I haven't done something like this in ages. But I think we should leave it at that. Let's go and have a curry. My supper earlier was cut rather short.'

Gus's hands remain on the back of the seats. 'They won't bite.'

Jim shakes his head. 'Michele and I are going through a bit of a rough patch, but I'm not up for a fling.'

'You sound like a frightened schoolboy.' Gus laughs. 'Marriage really does weird things to us men, eh? We are going to have a nice pleasant chat and invite them out for a meal. That's all. Take the chairs back and I'll buy us another round of drinks.'

Hanna and Natalie are from Poland. Jim met Natalie at the bar. She is a doctor at the Royal Free. Her friend Hanna works as a hairdresser and appears younger. Natalie has been in the UK for five years, while Hanna only arrived six months ago. They love hard rock. 'Like all Eastern Europeans,' Natalie laughs self-mockingly. Soon the conversation turns to Scotland. Gus was born and bred in Edinburgh, and the two women are planning a three-week summer break up in Scotland next month, island-hopping in the Hebrides. When the music starts up again, the invitation to the restaurant, this time made by Gus, feels natural, and Hanna and Natalie are clearly delighted to have met two admirers of Scotland.

The remains of Jim's initial trepidation are washed away with Indian lager. He sees Hanna's head flirtatiously fall on to Gus's shoulder. Gus's arm rests on the back of Hanna's chair. Natalie reaches for the water and, filling his glass, her hand briefly touches Jim's. A perfect little round birthmark sits in the middle of her right cheek.

They are the last to leave the restaurant. Outside, the air smells beautifully fresh and clean. Hanna has put her arm into Gus's. Natalie keeps both hands in the pockets of her jacket, but every few steps her arm brushes Jim's by chance.

'What would the ladies like to do now?' Gus asks.

'Let's go dancing,' Hanna says.

'Do you know a place?'

'Of course,' she assures him.

They take a taxi to a nightclub near Piccadilly. Thumping beat, flashing lights through darkness, twitching bodies. The smell of sweat and perfume and life and desire. And youth. Natalie's body touches Jim's on the dance floor. Her arms above her head. Their legs move into each other, their upper bodies brush and for moments sway in unison. Then she takes a step back and their eyes meet and Jim pulls her gently closer by the waist. Over her head, he sees Gus and Hanna kissing.

'Hanna and I are heading back to mine,' Gus says when they meet back at the table.

He sees Hanna talk to Natalie. Natalie replies, Hanna shakes her head, laughs.

Hanna turns back to Gus.

'My friend says I am not allowed to go on my own into a stranger's apartment. She is coming too.' She pauses, then taps Gus's nose with her index finger. 'But not that you get the wrong idea.'

In the taxi Gus entertains them with anecdotes about buying a French chateau. 'The deal is nearly concluded,' he says proudly. 'And then I will produce the best wine in the world. It's pretty good already, what they've been producing, but I will improve upon it.'

'We will taste the wine,' Hanna declares. 'I love French wine.'

Gus kisses her neck. 'Whatever you wish.'

Back at his flat, they open a bottle and taste the wine. Then they open another. Gus and Hanna have disappeared. Natalie snuggles up closer to Jim on the sofa. She puts her feet under his legs. Her mouth feels soft and warm and tastes of red wine.

CLARA – ONE YEAR LATER

I AM FINE on my own. I've always been fine on my own. I love the silence in the house. When Edward was still around and the children were at home I often couldn't wait until the door shut behind them. I then sat on the sofa with a coffee. Motionless. Enjoying the silence. Enjoying that no one made demands on me. I was busy sitting there, as I am always busy. Don't misunderstand me. I span my cocoon. I made it whole again. When people are around – even the ones I love dearly – my cocoon gets pierced with little tiny holes. And then they frighten me, because they can attack me through these holes. And sometimes they do indeed attack me. At least, they used to. When I still had to mingle with people because life wouldn't allow me to do otherwise. When the children were small, when Edward was around. I don't know why my cocoon is so porous. I don't even know if others have a cocoon at all. Need a cocoon. The moment I came in contact with people my cocoon would become brittle and I had to keep people at bay. I didn't want them to peep through the holes, to see me naked. Of course, most people didn't want to do me any harm. But their mere presence pierced holes. And they came too close.

Mending the delicate fabric of the cocoon took a lot of effort and time. That's what I used to do when I sat on the sofa for hours. I didn't have a rocking chair. Even a rocking chair would have caused too much turbulence. You can't mend a delicate fabric while in motion. It requires careful needlework. Painstakingly picking up the stitches with a very fine needle. I unplugged the telephone and didn't answer the door for the postman. I needed the silence, the safety of my four walls around me. I still do. But I have become better. Perhaps all the mending and repairing has led to the cocoon being stuck, being sewn to my skin. And my skin has turned into leather. And now I am finally thick-skinned.

I miss Edward. Edward was my link to the outside world. I felt safe with him. He wasn't scared of people; he could handle them. I wasn't always kind to him, but he forgave me and that was a nice feeling. In bed

I used to put my head on his shoulder and my feet underneath his feet. It didn't matter how angry I had been during the day. He died in the middle of the night. He simply slipped away. I must have noticed something because I turned around and put my arm around him and knew straight away that he wasn't breathing any longer. I didn't move. I closed my eyes and breathed for the two of us. The morning came and I still didn't move. As long as I stayed in bed nothing had changed.

The silence after his departure was different. More absolute, of course. Initially I worried that I might feel lonely. But I didn't. Loneliness has never bothered me. Loneliness for me is something beautiful. It means the absence of danger. The absence of danger of being attacked. Why then did I become so angry when I was lying at the bottom of the stairs in Rose Gardens? So angry that I couldn't get up. Anger overcomes me in a blind rage. It overcomes me when I suddenly see myself from the outside and I see a lonely, old, batty woman and I think this shouldn't be. What this? My situation, my status, my circumstances. From the outside a lonely old woman should be cared for, looked after. And so I insist and demand because I know that anyone looking onto the scene from the outside shakes their head and says, This shouldn't be. I forget myself, I forget who I am, that silence and loneliness are my haven. It doesn't make me feel lonely.

Michele's house makes me feel lonely. I walk around in it. I know every corner, every drawer, every slip of paper laying around.

And I found the four black bin liners stuffed with Jim's clothes.

They are the bin liners I have seen in my dream. And I thought it was me who was throwing Edward on to the rubbish heap. No. Michele has thrown Jim on to the rubbish heap. I sat down on her bed and stared at the four black bin bags in her wardrobe. Why hasn't he come to pick them up? Why hasn't she taken them away? I closed the door and returned to my basement and sat on the rocking chair. And I rocked back and forth, back and forth.

And I cried for Michele.

I felt so sorry that I had seen those black bin liners. That I had laid eyes on them. That I had pierced her silence. I don't know why they broke up, whether he left her or she threw him out or they separated on mutual terms. All I know is that neither I nor anyone else should have laid eyes on those bin liners. They belong in my dreams, and there they should have stayed. I didn't have the right to create a situation where they materialized in reality.

I picked up the phone and dialled her mobile. Her voicemail came on. I put down the phone. For a moment I hesitated. Should I ring again and leave a message? But what did I want to say? I was sobbing. And the only words that came to mind were, I am sorry. I am sorry for the black bin liners in your wardrobe. I am sorry that I created a situation where the bin bags from my dream have turned up in your life. She wouldn't have understood. She doesn't understand such talk. She is far too pragmatic. She'd probably have listened impatiently and then, as soon as the telephone call was finished, she would have called Hilary or Larissa and told them to pass by and check on me. I don't need anyone to check on me, thank you very much. I have created mayhem. And I need to undo it. And I know what to do. Words won't mean anything in this situation. Perhaps one day, when all of this is over, I will be able to talk to Michele and say that I am sorry in a way that she will understand. Now there is no time to find the right words. Now I have things to do.

1 3

JIM IS LYING on his back. On a sofa. He opens his eyes. A blanket covers him. But this isn't his sofa. For a moment he is disorientated. Gus. Two women. Hanna and Natalie. His hands pad along his body. He is fully dressed. His belt is buckled, too. He moves his head in pain and immediately feels his stomach turn. He jumps up and rushes to the bathroom. Empty bottles and half-empty glasses on the low coffee table in the living room. The doors to the spare room and Gus's bedroom are closed. No sounds. There are women's cowboy boots on the floor, one underneath the table, the other in front of the sofa. Jim goes into the kitchen, noticing that he even kept his socks on. He pours himself a glass of water. The sun blazes in a clear blue sky outside the window. Quarter to eleven. He goes back to the sofa. He remembers kissing Natalie. He gulps down his water, stares at the empty glass in his hand. His hand is shaking. He hears the door to the spare room opening, then the bathroom door closing.

He should talk to her. Whatever happened last night, that's the least he can do. He hears the loo flushing. He turns his head and looks down the corridor. Her gaze is directed at the floor; she seems to be heading back to her room.

'Good morning,' Jim says.

Natalie looks up, while her hand reaches towards the door that she'd left ajar.

'Good morning.'

She is wearing a T-shirt and knickers. She squints.

'I can't really see you without contact lenses.' She laughs apologetically.

'Would you like a coffee?' Jim asks.

She doesn't reply immediately, appears to be hesitating. Then says, 'Yes, thank you.'

She disappears into the room. In the kitchen, Jim puts on the kettle.

14

I BUTTON MY coat and put on my hat. I bring my face close to the mirror. I put on some lipstick. Smack my lips.

I take my handbag. I open it to double-check: yes, the money is in there. I smile at myself in the mirror. I don't need to ask anyone for permission to find a place of my own because I have enough money to pay the first few months' rent up front. Straight away. I am sure no estate agent will refuse such an offer.

I close the door behind me, climb the few steps up to the pavement. It's such a beautiful day. And I do love to get out early in the morning. I ought to thank Michele. If she hadn't ordered her cab and the cab driver hadn't rung the doorbell, I wouldn't have woken up. I heard the doorbell and Michele's feet flying down the stairs, rushing along the corridor. The door opened; the door closed again. She went back upstairs. The cab driver left his engine running outside. I sat up, put on the light, turned it straight off again. I didn't want Michele to see the light. And anyway, I didn't need it. Dawn was creeping through the curtains. I looked for my glasses. Quarter past five. I was wide awake. Nevertheless, I must have gone back to sleep at some point because when I looked at the clock next it was nearly seven o'clock.

I turn left and walk down the street. I have a spring in my step. I'm feeling quite young again. I might have a coffee in Highgate. And once I've talked to the estate agent, I might venture into the West End. I'd love to look at some Greek vases at the British Museum. There was a programme about them on Radio 4 the other day. I wish Michele could have listened to it. About how vases represent the womb and women's need to recreate the womb. She's been sneering at my vases ever since I started. And I know that she's got a box full of them out in the garden shed. She forgot to hide them before I moved in. But the mother-and-child model stands on the mantelpiece in the living room.

Involuntarily, I laugh out loud while passing the nursing home. A nurse is sitting in the front garden, smoking a cigarette. I wave at her. Why not? She probably thinks that just because I am laughing out loud I'm mad. She'd love me to be inside that home, wouldn't she? Like a witch, a white witch, that's how she sits there in her front garden.

'This is a nursing home, Mum, where elderly people go to recuperate after an operation or a long illness,' Michele explained, sounding like a schoolmistress talking to a dumb child. 'They stay for a few weeks, then they leave. What Hilary and I have chosen for you is a home where elderly people live together.'

I wish she'd stop saying 'elderly'. And I wish she'd stop trying to pull the wool over my eyes. That's how it works in the business world. But not with me.

I turn right, up the hill. Pah, I need to slow down. I stop, slightly out of breath. Panting. I touch a garden wall with my right hand, put my left hand against my heart. Breathe . . . breathe. My lips tremble. Should I turn back? I have caught my breath. I look up into the blue sky. I will continue to walk. The fresh air is doing me good. Old people don't recuperate after an operation or a long illness. Old people start dying. And no one wants to see them dying nowadays. I looked after Mutti right up to the end. And I would have taken her into my house, but Edward was against the idea. So I

drove to Norwich three, sometimes four, times a week.
Hilary had just finished school. I was thinking about
taking some drawing classes. I even got prospectuses.
But then Mutti's health deteriorated.

I've reached the top of the hill. There is this
lovely block of flats here. I stop and look up to the
top floor. It was built before the war and reminds
me of home, of Germany. I suddenly know that's
where I want to live. On the sixth floor. Beth lived
here. I'd forgotten about her. I wonder if she's still
around. But it's too early to knock on her door and
I can't remember her flat number anyway. Though
I once visited her for coffee when Michele was a
baby. Before we moved to Battersea. The view across
London is breathtaking. Yes, that's where I am going
to live. High up in the sky. Not hidden away in a
basement. I open my bag and touch my money. I'm
so lucky to have my savings. I now hurry. I want to
be the first at the estate agent's. I want to be there
as soon as they open. So that no one else can snatch
away my flat from in front of my nose. It's such a big
block of flats. Surely one of the estate agents will
have a flat available.

I am crossing the bridge and throw a quick glance to
the left. The hills beyond London are visible. But I have

no time to contemplate the scenery. I've got business
to attend to this morning. I cross the road at the traffic
lights. The pavement on the park side is shady. It will
give me some respite from the sun. I can feel my heart
thumping and working hard. I don't know what time it
is. But I left the house at eight, so surely it's not even
nine yet. And those estate agents won't open before
nine thirty at the earliest. I've already made it halfway
up Highgate Hill. The gate to the park is open. I might
as well take a short break. I enter the park. I pass the
first few benches. They are too close to the road. You
can still hear the traffic. Eventually I find the ideal
spot. In the shade, looking south over a vast open
green space.

I sit down on the bench. I am now truly out of
breath. I loosen the top button of my coat. I am quite
hot from walking. I open my bag to see if I can find
something – a pamphlet, a piece of paper – to fan
myself with. No. I take out my handkerchief and
by accident pull out a few banknotes too. I quickly
grab the ones that have fallen on to the bench and stuff
them back into my bag. I notice a couple that have
fallen on to the path. I will collect them in a moment.
But let me first catch my breath. I dab my forehead

with the handkerchief and wipe some drops of sweat from my upper lip. That feels better. I close my eyes.

Someone has joined me on the bench. I open my eyes and turn my head. I'm pleased to see an old man. Probably around my age, I'd say. For a split second I was worried that it might be someone about to take my money. This man looks harmless. Though he does smell.

'Morning, young lady. Could you spare me a pound?'

No manners! How about some small talk first! My eyes search the ground around my feet for the banknotes. There aren't any. I frown. Surely no one could have picked them up. I had my eyes closed for a minute or two at most and would have noticed anyone scrabbling about down by my feet. Perhaps I made a mistake. After all, tiny beads of sweat had been running into my eyes.

My hands are about to tighten around the bag in my lap, when I notice it isn't in my lap. It's standing next to me. Open. I snatch it and press it tight against my chest, shaking my head vehemently from side to side.

'OK, OK, lady. Don't get upset. I've asked for an act

of kindness from you, but if you can't spare a penny for an old man . . .'

He gets up mid-sentence and simply walks off. I stare at him, hugging my bag so hard that my arms start to hurt. Then I loosen my grip.

15

'MILK AND SUGAR?'

As Jim pushes the plunger of the cafetière down and Natalie pushes her cup silently across the table towards him, Jim suddenly realizes that he has forgotten to put out either. At home, Michele and he drink black coffee.

'No, thank you.'

Natalie lifts her cup, blows on the steaming liquid and takes a small sip. She has tied her hair back in a ponytail and is wearing glasses that make her look more serious than she did last night. He can imagine her as a doctor now.

'I hope you didn't misunderstand me last night,' she says hesitantly as she lowers her cup again. Her eyes are fixed on a spot on the table. 'This doesn't usually happen to me.'

Again, Jim's stomach slightly turns. He swallows and hopes that he doesn't need to rush to the bathroom. For a moment he closes his eyes.

'I am sorry,' he says.

'For what?' She now looks up and straight into his eyes.

'For last night.'

A smile hovers around her lips. 'You behaved impeccably.'

He averts his eyes and lifts the cup to his mouth to disguise his confusion. He is making a fool of himself.

'So what happened last night?' He looks back across the table at her.

'We kissed.' She pauses, then says, 'I wanted you. And you wanted me. But then you stopped and told me that you are married.'

A buzzing fly has appeared in the kitchen. It knocks against the closed window. A silence follows, but only for a few seconds before the buzzing starts again.

'And then?'

Jim wishes he could remember. But his last memory is of being on the sofa kissing her. She is beautiful. Now with a slight hangover and no make-up, even more so, because it is a less self-conscious beauty.

For a brief moment she holds his gaze.

'You went to the bathroom. But before that you insisted I should take the bed in the spare room.'

She stands up and opens the window. The fly immediately finds its way out and disappears. She turns towards him with a smile.

'You stayed in the bathroom for quite a while. I sat on the bed in the spare room waiting for the bathroom to become available. Eventually I got worried and knocked on the door. But no reply. Not a sound. So I opened the door and there you were, sitting on the floor with your back against the bathtub, fast asleep.'

Jim senses the heat rising from his stomach into his face. But seeing her cheeky smile, he laughs.

'I can handle a couple of beers happily, but anything more . . . I am truly embarrassed.'

'It was rather cute seeing this big man fast asleep on the floor. I had to help you up, then covered you with a blanket on the sofa.' She shuts the window.

'I enjoyed yesterday evening. If you weren't married . . .'

'I can smell coffee.' Gus has suddenly appeared in the doorway.

Jim glances at Natalie briefly, then turns his attention to his friend.

'Good morning.'

Gus has thrown on a pair of trackies and an old T-shirt. Jim pushes back his chair.

'I need to go, but I'll put on some more coffee.'

Gus disappears into the bathroom. Natalie's chair scrapes along the linoleum behind Jim. He turns around. She comes towards him. Then stops. He reaches out for her and pulls her close. Her cheek rests against his shoulder, her face turned away. He feels her breathing, her heart beat. She moves, he loosens his grip. Quietly, she closes the door of the spare room behind her. Her smell lingers on his body.

The bright sun hits him squarely in the face. The Heath is heaving with joggers and children and dogs and young parents. He walks quickly, with his hands in his trouser pockets and his gaze low, hoping not to meet anyone he knows. He tries to remember the conversation from last night. But again he can't summon up much except lots of laughter and enjoying himself, but feeling out of place and an odd sensation of missing Michele, but not the Michele he had left in anger at home. He falls into a light trot and fills his lungs with air. His head begins to clear. His body feels strong. Michele and he should do something together. Get away from the house. Perhaps even away from London. They could drive up to Norfolk and walk along the beach, book into a B&B.

16

I'VE BEEN SITTING on this park bench for quite a while now. The man frightened me. Perhaps I shouldn't talk alone to an estate agent. I look at the closed handbag in my lap. I don't want to open it again. When I snatched at it a few minutes ago, an empty space inside flashed past my eyes before the bag snapped shut beneath my fingers. I am sure no one could have taken the money. But I prefer not to check for the moment. I will ask Hilary to accompany me to the estate agent's later on. However, she usually comes mid-morning, so I have a bit of time to kill. I don't want to go home just yet. Having made it this far I might as well walk to the Heath. I stand up. My back and knees are hurting. I have got cold and stiff on the bench. I walk slowly towards the south exit of the park, near the cemetery. A group of school-children are rushing past in the opposite direction. A dog chases after a ball on the grass. I stop and look at the dog. Memories of Vicky come flooding back, a

lovely dog and such a loyal, simple soul. Hilary named
her Vicky. With her long furry ears and tappity feet,
Vicky looked and behaved like a dog who thought she
was the luckiest creature in the world. She jumped
along rather than ran. I decide to sit down again and
watch the dog. A woman with a pushchair stands at
the edge of the grass. She rolls the pushchair back and
forth. The dog arrives with the ball, she lets go of the
pushchair, holds out her hand and the dog drops the
ball into her palm. It is sitting down on its haunches,
beating the grass with its tail and looking up at its
owner, barely able to contain its excitement in antici-
pation of the next throw. But the woman keeps the
ball in her hand. She drops it into the bag that dangles
over the handles of the pushchair. She says something
to the dog, which immediately jumps up and charges
ahead. The woman follows slowly. I watch them until
they disappear around the next bend. Then I stand up.

For a split second the world vanishes behind a
black screen. Small sparkling stars pierce the darkness. The ground beneath my feet is spinning. I must
have stood up too quickly. I drop back on to the bench.
I feel the wood of the seat under my hand and stability
returns. I am still holding the handkerchief crumpled
up in my hand. Once again I dab the perspiration off

my face. It would be lovely to have a wet handkerchief
to cool my face, my neck. It would be lovely to have
some water to drink, too. I could shuffle back up the
hill towards Highgate. There are shops and cafés. But
the hill is quite steep. My body suddenly remembers
the feeling of pushing the pram up it. One child inside
– must have been Hilary – and the other one sitting
on it in one of these removable seats. And the prams
in those days were heavy. No, going back up the hill
would mean I won't make it to the Heath today. But I
would really love to reach it. My mouth is dry. There
are no shops between here and the Heath. How silly.
The middle of London and no shops. I close my eyes.
It's lovely to sit in the shade. A cool breeze touches
my cheeks. It's a pity Edward isn't here any longer. I
could have put my head against his shoulder. And we
could have stayed here and rested. Anyway. I shouldn't
waste time. I push myself up and walk out of the park.
My feet are as heavy as lead. I can barely lift them. But
after a while it becomes easier. My arms feel light now,
they are dangling by my side. I carry no handbag. For a
split second I hesitate mid-stride. Then the decision is
made. I won't turn back. I don't want to know if there
is anything in the bag or not. I chuckle as I imagine
that handbag so lonely on the bench. Did I take my

handkerchief? My hand slips into my coat pocket. Yes, it's there. That's all I need. What do I need a bag for anyway? I never liked bags. My hand rises up to my head. And I never liked hats either. I pull the pillbox hat off. Silly, silly stupid hat. I balance it on a branch hanging right over the pavement from a front-garden hedge. I don't care if anyone is looking. It's dangling in the wind, that silly old hat. Once again I can't help chuckling, then I make a straight face and go on my way.

A man is watering plants in a garden.

'Excuse me, young man, would you mind giving me a glass of water? I am rather thirsty.'

The man turns around and sees a little old lady, quite pale, with beads of sweat on her forehead. Her light-blue trench coat is half unbuttoned. She looks slightly deranged and he wonders if she should be out on her own. Perhaps he should call an ambulance. I know that's what he's thinking. I can read his mind.

'Would you like to come in and sit down while I fetch you a glass of water?'

'Oh no. That's very kind of you. Thank you. But I'd rather stay here.'

Don't ever go into the house of a stranger, Mutti told me. I catch myself just in time not to say it out

loud. The man already looks quite bewildered and if I
say this he will surely think I am away with the fairies.
A batty old woman. Well, I am not batty, that's for sure.
I take a deep breath. I feel alive. As alive as a naughty
little girl who has finally got rid of a silly pillbox hat
and a useless handbag. I feel even better after drinking
the water. Water is something beautiful, isn't it? I will
go swimming in the pond, the ladies' pond. Yes, that's
what I am going to do. I thank the young man and as
I turn away I catch him bending down to pick up his
watering can, holding his back. No longer that young.
I unbutton my coat and put my hands in my pockets.

I am wearing three-quarter length trousers and
flat black pumps. My coat is black too. My long ponytail à la Brigitte Bardot is swaying from left to right as
I am heading through the Latin Quarter to the atelier
where I am working. Glue and clay from yesterday are
still stuck beneath my fingernails and I can't wait to
return to the piece.

I take off my coat and hang it over a fence.

I see myself stopping at the café just around the
corner from the atelier. I order a café au lait at the
bar and a croissant and light a cigarette. The patron
knows me and knows I don't talk much.

I cross the road and walk towards the Heath. I

stop and hesitate. Where is the ladies' pond? It's
been a long time since I came here. Edward eventually wanted to move back to south London. It was the
area where he grew up, that he knew best. I missed
the green of the hilly north. Mind you, I never swam
in the pond. And I only visited it once, with Edward's
sister, who's dead now too. I've never learned to swim
properly. Michele goes swimming there all the time.
She loves it, it invigorates her, she says.

'Can I help you?'

A woman stands in front of me.

'Tell me, dear, where is the ladies' pond?'

'Would you like the quickest way?'

'Yes, please.'

'You follow this road along the edge of the Heath.
In about five minutes, you come to a gravel path. Take
the path for a couple of minutes and then you'll see
the entrance to the pond on your left.'

'Thank you.'

I nod and, before the woman has time to say anything else, I walk briskly in the direction she indi-
cated. I am suddenly in a hurry to get to the pond. But
after a few metres I slow down again. I look back over
my shoulder. The woman is no longer there. Thank
God. Somehow I didn't like the look of her at all. The

concerned gaze in her eyes. Pah, anyway, what do I care? I stretch my hand out and let my fingers brush past the hazel hedges hanging over the iron railings that separate the edge of the Heath from this small narrow road.

I am entering my atelier, dropping my coat carelessly on the only chair and approaching the big lump of clay in the middle of the room. It might be totally dried out. I don't yet know what the last few hours have done to it. I worked fast yesterday till late at night, constantly hosing it down to keep it as moist as possible. I was soaked to the bone too but continued to work. From the beginning I knew I wanted to keep on working after daylight had gone. To incorporate the passage of time, day and night, the difference between seeing and feeling. One day I will work with a huge lump of clay far away from any electric light. Somewhere in the deepest French south. But that is not an option at the moment. I have to stay here in Paris. My teachers are here. I am learning a lot. I step up to the clay. The tip of my nose is touching it. The plastic sheet rustles. I close my eyes, then move to put my cheek against the clay. I open my arms and embrace it. My hands don't touch on the other side. The object resembles a cone. The base is much wider than the top, which reaches about half a metre above my head. I spread my legs wide and push my feet along the floor around the base as far as possible without losing my balance. Then I press my body against the clay. My breasts, my tummy, my pelvis. 'Let's get to work, you and I,' I whisper. I let go and start to loosen the rope that I used to keep the plastic sheet in place. I have no idea what is awaiting me. I could have continued working last night. But I didn't. I wanted to incorporate sleep. Time advancing while I was sleeping. Time passing without me seeing or touching my object. What would time left to its own devices do to my object? I pull down the plastic sheet.

I have reached the path. The gravel beneath my feet crunches. It's beautifully cool here under the shade of the big old horse chestnut trees. Like being in a huge dark forest. Mutti always warned me not to come to the Heath alone. I took her once and she didn't like the dark parts overgrown with trees at all. Strangers might be lurking. I lean my head back. The sunbeams filtering through the leaves touch my face.

17

JIM OPENS THE door. He is met by the smell of freshly brewed coffee, but he receives no answer when he calls out to Michele. In the kitchen he sees her coffee cup on the table next to an empty plate. He turns and heads upstairs. The bed hasn't yet been made. Her laptop is on her desk in the study with the lid closed. He returns to the kitchen and approaches the kitchen table. A large sheet of paper is covering one side.

Michele finds a parking spot right outside the house. She takes two of the flowerpots out of the boot, one in each arm.

She walks into the house and sees Jim standing in the kitchen, his hands on the edge of the table, leaning forward, supporting his weight with his arms. The sudden realization that she didn't tidy away the plans for the basement conversion before she rushed out of the house makes her freeze mid-step.

'What's this?' Jim asks without looking up.

Michele starts moving again and places the two pots on the kitchen counter and her shoulder bag next to it. She takes the keyring out of her mouth.

'Preliminary drawings for converting the basement into a separate flat,' she replies.

She moves towards him. The sleeves of his shirt are rolled up. Thick, blue veins protrude. He is unshaven, his shirt and his trousers creased.

'I can explain. It's not what you think it is.'

She places her hand on his upper arm. He doesn't look up. She removes her hand.

'I'll just fetch the remaining flowerpots from the car,' she says.

'What's this?' Jim repeats, trying to collect his thoughts. Who is betraying whom here? She takes him for granted. She disregards his opinions. She behaves as if they weren't sharing a life. And he is idiotically loyal.

Michele stops in the doorway. The front door is standing wide open. A man with a white Fox Terrier walks past.

'We can talk about it. No decision has been made yet.'

She is about to turn on her heel again when she

hears Jim slowly saying, 'Oh yes, a decision has been made,' enunciating each word clearly and with emphasis. He picks up the sheet of paper and rips it down the middle. 'As long as I live in this house, the basement will not be converted.' He puts the drawings on the table, then thumps the table with his fist.

Michele flinches, hesitates, then heads outside to lock the car. She will fetch the other flowerpots later. Stepping back into the house, she closes the front door behind her. In the hallway Jim walks straight past her and climbs the stairs. An unfamiliar, sweet smell follows him.

'Where were you last night?' Michele asks calmly.

Jim continues up the stairs. At the top, he turns the corner and disappears from sight. She catches up with him in their bedroom as he is pulling his shirt over his head. She inhales. The smell of a sickeningly-sweet woman's perfume hangs in the air. She stares at his naked torso. He goes to the gym regularly. He plays cricket during the summer and practises indoors during the winter.

'Where were you last night?' she asks again.

His head reappears. He looks her straight in the face, letting the shirt drop on to the bed.

'Giving you a reason not to trust me,' he says calmly.

'What do you mean?'

'You know exactly what I mean.' He unbuckles his belt.

'You are lying.'

He picks up the shirt from the bed and throws it at her. She catches it spontaneously.

'Smell it.'

She holds the shirt in her hands but doesn't bring it up to her nose. It smells of his sweat and the sweet perfume.

'You are lying,' she repeats.

He unzips his trousers.

'Why should I?' He shrugs and lets the trousers drop to the floor, stepping out of them and picking them up with one foot, kicking them on to the bed.

'I've never lied to you.'

He drops his underpants and kicks them on to the bed too.

'Don't be ridiculous,' Michele says between gritted teeth, the shirt still in her hands.

Jim now stands fully naked in front of her.

'I have indeed been a ridiculous fool. For twenty-five years.' He pauses, then adds, 'I would like to take a shower.'

'So you fucked another woman.'

Jim watches his wife's lips, which have become a tense straight line.

'If you have any decency left, you will at least answer that question,' she adds.

'I didn't think you asked me a question,' Jim replies. 'It sounded like one of your usual statements. No need for me to add my version of events.'

He pushes past Michele and leaves the room. She doesn't move. The dust is dancing in the sunbeams that fall through the window. The glass is covered in smears. She needs to tell her cleaner to take more care.

'Who?' she asks.

In reply to her question she hears the gushing water of the shower. She drops the shirt. Jim is standing in front of the shower, feeling the water.

'Who?' she repeats.

He steps underneath the shower. He closes his eyes, leans his head back, pointing his face upwards. Michele steps inside the wet room, reaches out to the shower handle and turns the water off.

'I think we should talk.'

'Switch the shower back on, Michele.'

Jim hasn't opened his eyes. He feels his way to the handle blindly. Michele hasn't moved her hand. He opens his eyes and turns towards his wife.

'I advise you to leave the room.'

'I am not leaving until you give me an answer.'

'Michele, I am asking you one last time: please leave the room.'

She shakes her head. For a moment they both stare at each other. Then Jim grabs Michele's shoulders and pushes her towards the door, holding on to her.

'Get out!' he screams into her face. With the force of his body weight he pushes her out of the shower room. The door slams shut. He locks it from the inside.

She stands outside the closed door. She hears the water running. She hears his phone ringing in the kitchen. For a split second she hesitates. Then she rushes down the stairs. An unknown number. She picks up the phone.

'Hello? Jim?' A woman's voice with a foreign accent.

'This is his wife speaking,' Michele says. Silence. Michele hears the other woman breathing. Then the line is cut.

'Do you mind?' Jim stands in front of her, with a towel around his waist, water dripping from his hair and body on to the floor. He holds out his hand with an immobile face. Michele places the phone into his hand. They look at each other. Stone-faced.

'If you call her back,' Michele says quietly, 'we will no longer live under one roof.'

She turns and walks out of the room.

'Natalie, it's Jim.'

Michele touches the banister as the kitchen door swings shut. Jim's muffled laugh from behind the door reaches her ear. She goes into the study and sits down at her desk.

18

I AM STANDING at the edge of the jetty, looking down into the water. My shoes in my hand. Tights in my skirt pocket. It's been such a long time since my bare feet have felt the sun. I wiggle my toes. I can't wait to go on to the grass. I will change outside. Not go into that stuffy changing room. I remember some women changing outside all those years ago, when I once came to the pond but didn't dare go into the water because I was scared of its depth. I looked away quickly when I saw those naked bodies. I felt embarrassed for them. Now I can't wait. If only they would allow us to jump into the pond naked. But it's forbidden. I look around. The young lifeguard has disappeared inside the changing room to search for a spare swimming costume for me. They always have some spare ones, she told me, the ones people have forgotten. What if I just slipped out of my clothes and simply jumped in? I giggle like a little girl at the mere thought of it. The sun makes me so giddy. I would swim out into the middle of the pond and the lifeguard could stand here and shout as much as she likes. By the time I reached the middle of the pond, I'd probably not hear anything. My hearing has worsened considerably in the last few months. I'd swim front crawl. I can't remember if I have ever swum front crawl before. Most likely not. I'm not very good at swimming. But I have watched it on the television a lot. The slow-motion bit. I love the way the arm comes out of the water at an angle and the swimmer effortlessly glides along. I will take swimming lessons. Yes, that's what I will do. Here at the pond each morning. I drop my shoes on to the jetty and stretch my arms over my head. It's such a beautiful morning.

'I've found you a couple.'

The young woman has returned and holds out a purple swimming costume and a black one. I let my arms drop to my sides and stretch out my hand for the purple one.

'You are sweet. Thank you. I'll change over there.' I point to the empty grass slope on the right.

'There are a couple of towels people have left behind too.'

'No, don't you worry.' I shake my head. 'I love lying on the grass.'

I bend down to pick up my shoes and notice that

neither my knee nor my hip pains me. I straighten up
with ease and flash a smile at the woman. As I step on
to the gravel path the soles of my feet hurt at first, but
then I simply quicken my step, almost dancing along.
Walking in the early morning does me good. I reach the
grass. How beautifully soft and cool and moist. Where
should I position myself? There is a small slope, with
old trees and hedges at the top shielding the pond
from the public path. It's shadowy up there. The rest of
the grass bank is bathed in beautiful morning sunlight.
I head right for the middle. I want to feel openness all
around me. I sit down and fall backwards, stretching
my arms and legs out like a starfish. Then I move my
arms up and down and close and open my legs. I am
making an angel – a grass angel – like I used to do in
the snow – a snow angel. I can't remember when I last
made an angel. It must have been before we left home.
With my best friend, Frauke. Who died before we left.
The damp is penetrating my clothes.

'*Clara, steh auf, du holst dir eine Nierenentzündung.*
Clara, get up, you will catch nephritis.'

I stop moving, look to the left and then to the right.
Green grass and the sound of birds. I look up into the
blue sky.

'Mutti, you are no longer here. Leave me alone.'

And I am lying very still, listening. Mutti has gone away. And I laugh out loud and continue moving my arms and legs. I am making a beautiful angel with a very clear outline that will stay in the grass for a long time. I suddenly stop and sit up.

You silly old woman, I say out loud. But I am not actually angry with myself. I am far too happy. I stand up. My back and behind have got a bit damp after all. But I have never in my life caught nephritis and won't catch it now either. I have a lovely view over the pond. I can see the jetty and the lifeguard's hut. The young woman is sitting inside. I squint. I can't see the far end of the pond from here, because it is hidden behind trees. I start walking to the right. A wooden fence runs along the edge of the grass bank and separates it from the lake. How silly that humans continuously need to shield and protect. And separate places where you are allowed to swim from those where you are not. And where you are allowed to be naked from where you are not. How silly, silly, silly. I lean over the fence to see how far it reaches into the bushes. It seems to be going all the way. Further along, towards the far end of the lake, I spot an old wooden jetty poking out into the water from the hedge. It is hidden behind trees and leads right into the reeds. I straighten up and look over to the lifeguard's hut. No, she won't be able to see me once I disappear into the bushes. I will climb over the fence from there. I cast a quick glance back to my shoes and the swimming costume lying forlorn on the grass next to the angel with the widespread wings. I turn and walk into the thicket.

The jetty is now right in front of me on the other side of the fence. There is a gate, but it is locked with a big iron padlock. The fence reaches nearly to my chest. I've never climbed a fence. Not ever. This will be the first time. I put both feet on the wooden plank that runs horizontally a few inches off the ground. The fence posts are pointed. My only chance to get over is to lift one of my legs high enough to step on to the top horizontal bar, then pull the other foot up and jump. Yesterday I wouldn't have even dared to contemplate this. Now I just do it. I lift my foot, place it on the upper bar and for a moment I am so surprised at myself that I stop breathing. I want to laugh. Wait, I remind myself. You haven't yet reached the other side. Concentration is required. I'm not sure how to proceed from here. So I simply hold on to the pointed fence posts, lean forward and pull up my other leg. For a split second I balance on top of the fence, and all I know is that I mustn't lean back, otherwise I will fall

[123]

on to the wrong side. I lean even further forward. And fall head first. I lie still, very still, and wait for the pain.

No pain. Still I don't move. I might be dead. Then my hands become aware of the moist ground beneath my palms and I know I am alive, and I smell the dark soil and gather some in my fist and bring it close to my nose. I sprinkle it on my face and laugh, and I put out my tongue and taste the earth. I have climbed a fence and it was so easy. I will do it again and again and again. I sit up. Why have I never climbed a fence before? Perhaps I never wanted something badly enough on the other side. I suddenly fall silent and hold my breath. Has anyone noticed? Two ducks appear from under the old jetty and swim out into the lake. The sun dances on the water. I stand up and unbutton my blouse, letting it slide down my back on to the ground. I unclip my bra, my arms bending backwards up my back as if I were a young woman. I unzip my skirt, push my pants down, hop over pants and skirt. I look down at myself. I have not looked in a mirror while naked for a long time. Wrinkly, baggy skin is not a pretty sight. But now as I am looking at myself I am oddly surprised. Yes, my breasts and my tummy are hanging; my skin looks baggy. I am an old woman, after all. But it is not ugly. This is skin that tells of experience and life. After my swim I will hurry home and translate this sight, me looking down at myself, into clay. A rush of enthusiasm floods my body. I finally know what my next piece of work will be. I fold my hands in front of my tummy and lift my face up to the sky. And I breathe in life and the blue sky. Then I step on to the wooden jetty. It looks rotten. Will it hold me? The jetty moves. I stop mid-stride. I hear birds in the tree behind me. I see a blue dragonfly dancing around my ankles. I feel the warm planks beneath my feet. With a firm step I walk to the edge of the jetty. I bend my knees, take my arms back, then bring them forward in one go and jump in head first. I feel the arc through the air, my hands breaking the surface of the water, my head, my body entering. For a moment the cold paralyses me and I wonder if my heart has stopped, but my legs and arms are already kicking, and I am heading up to the surface of the water. No. I take control of my movements, turn and start swimming underwater. My eyes are still closed. I feel the cold on my head, my breasts, between my legs, my hands, my feet. I stretch out and glide. Little bubbles escape from my mouth. I climbed a fence; I jumped into the water naked. Will I be courageous enough to open my eyes? It will be very dark. The pond is deep and very murky. I keep my arms still, my legs still. I open my eyes. Rays of light break through in total silence. My eye catches a ray. Where will it end? I have enough breath.

19

THE LITTLE BOY climbs up on the bench. He sits dangling his feet. His mum stands a bit further along the path. She is chatting on the phone but has her three-year-old in view out of the corner of her eye. An old lady in a light-blue summer coat and a matching pillbox hat sits at the other edge of the bench. She doesn't seem to mind the child.

'Why is your handbag open?' the little boy eventually asks.

The old lady doesn't reply. She has her eyes closed, her hands folded in her lap. For a few moments the boy returns to watching his dangling feet, until his curiosity gets the better of him. He peeps into the bag. It is empty.

'Why is your bag empty?' Again there is no reply.

'Rory, we have to go home, darling. It's lunchtime soon,' his mum calls.

He jumps down from the bench. As he climbs into the buggy, he says, 'The old lady doesn't like talking and she has an empty handbag.'

It takes a few seconds for the woman to process her son's words. Her mind was somewhere else. Then she looks over to the bench and sees the old woman sitting there very still. She doesn't appear to have moved at all. Her son is now back in the buggy. She fastens his seat belt. Home is in the opposite direction. She is about to turn the buggy but then changes her mind and approaches the bench.

She calls an ambulance and waits until the paramedics arrive. The old woman looks very peaceful. The paramedics confirm that she seems to have died about an hour ago. Probably of a heart attack. It's very likely she didn't even notice.

'A lovely way to go,' one of the paramedics says, smiling.

20

MICHELE – EIGHTEEN MONTHS LATER

FOUR BULGING BLACK bin liners. Jim never collected them. I guess at the beginning there wasn't enough space in Gus's spare bedroom. I don't want them in the flat when the children are coming for Christmas tomorrow. I quietly open the door, carry one bag after the other along the corridor to the elevator. I could have got rid of them as I was moving, along with Mum's and Dad's clothes. But I didn't.

The lights on the Christmas tree in the foyer are blinking forlornly. It's just gone 5 a.m. on Christmas Eve. The world is still asleep. I pull out the woollen hat, scarf and gloves I stuffed into my shoulder bag. Then I put the notice I have written on top of the bags, just to be on the safe side. 'Please don't remove. Fetching the car and will pick them up in 5 min.' The cold air hits me in the face. It is freezing. The digital thermometer in the car shows -6° Celsius. The winters are definitely turning colder and the summers hotter. I drive the car to the front of the block and load the bags into the boot. I will leave the clothes outside a charity shop in Battersea. I don't want to bring them to a shop in Highgate or Crouch End. I wouldn't want anyone to recognize Jim's clothes or to meet someone on the street who is wearing them.

I reach Waterloo Bridge in no time. Though I am surprised about the traffic on the road. I expected less. I cross Waterloo Bridge. I join the roundabout at the end, get into the lane to take the turning to carry me west. Then I suddenly change my mind. I won't take them to Battersea. There are still people I know and who know me. A car behind me hoots as I change lane. I drive around the roundabout to gather my thoughts. I want Jim's clothes where I am certain that no one knows me and no one knows him. I head south. I pass the Old Vic, and beyond that I don't know London at all. After a while I slow down, concentrating on the row of shops to my left. There is an Oxfam shop. I don't stop. I don't want a shop on the main road. I turn off left. Within a second I realize I made a mistake. I am now in a residential road and it's a one-way system and there are no shops; there will be no shops. I wait for a turning, then another turning, then I am back on the main road. But I am not heading south. I am heading back home. The roads are still clear and I get back to the flat at six twenty. I carry the bags inside. I take off my coat. I put the kettle on. While the water is boiling I dust Mum's clay model, which is standing on the mantelpiece in the living room. I dust it every day. It's my tribute to Mum. I make the coffee.

In the bedroom is a big wardrobe. It came with the flat. It is far too big for my clothes alone. I start to reorganize them. After an hour they have all found space behind the three doors on the left-hand side. The right side holds a rail, a few shelves and three big drawers. It's a beautiful wardrobe. Whoever designed it thought things through and knew what they were doing. I carry the bags from the hallway into the bedroom. Outside, dawn is slowly breaking. The sky displays a leaden grey colour. I open the bags and pile Jim's clothes on the bed. I refold them carefully before I put them into the wardrobe. Afterwards his smell lingers in the room. I turn off the lights and lie down on the bed. His clothes won't stay in the wardrobe for ever.

THANK YOU

I'd like to thank the women writers' retreat Hedgebrook on Whidbey Island, Washington, where I spent two wonderful weeks in the summer of 2012 working on this book.